NEW YORK TO MONTANA

DAN SULLIVAN
WITH **THOM SHEPHERD**
AND **ZACH NYTOMT**

New York to Montana

© 2019 by Old Stone Publishing

All rights reserved. No part of this book may be reproduced in any form or by any electronic or mechanical means, including information storage retrieval systems, stone tablets, sky writing, or tattooed on the cleavage of a pretty woman, without written permission from the publisher or author, except in the case of a reviewer, who may quote brief passages embodied in critical articles or in a review.

Published on a barstool in the U.S.A by:

Old Stone Publishing
Boise, ID 83714
info@oldstonepublishing.com
First Edition
ISBN: 9781792771446

Printed in the United States of America

All characters in this publication are entirely fictitious. Any resemblance to real persons, living or dead, is purely coincidental, unless you recognize yourself within the story in which case we will deny ever knowing you. Photos of us hanging out together in compromising situations doesn't strengthen your case in a court of law...we hope.

Dedicated to all those hardworking troubadours who appear on stage nightly hoping to see just one person in the audience who knows the words to a song they wrote with all of their heart and all of their soul.

FOREWORD

One of the great benefits of my job is that I get to travel the globe and meet lots of amazing people. In the last few years I've had the opportunity to meet both fellow musician, Zach Nytomt and author Dan Sullivan. I had no idea at the time the collision course these meetings would have or the amazing impact our collective imaginations might make on the world of words and music

After 9/11, I thought to myself, what if someone was supposed to be in the Twin Towers that morning, but maybe they were running late to work and saw the Towers fall? If they never came home that day, everyone would assume they had perished in the collapse of the buildings. And what if that person had a reason to disappear?

I first met songwriter Zach Nytomt at a Trinity Oaks event (check out trinityoaks.org) down in Port Mansfield, TX. Trinity Oaks take wounded veterans on a hunting and fishing trip as a thank you for their service to our country. Zach and I were the evening campfire entertainment for the trip, along with a few other guys. When my buddy John Michael Whitby introduced me to Zach, I said "What did you say your last name was again?" He said "Nytomt. It's like New York to Montana. You know, NY TO MT."

The wheels in my songwriter brain suddenly engaged and that 9/11 idea I had came rushing back to me. I thought, what if the guy disappearing from New York escapes to Montana? What if he leaves behind his stockbroker life and becomes a ranch hand or something? I told Zach my idea and over the next two years or so when we could get together we hashed out the song.

Shortly after Zach recorded the song in the summer of 2018 I ran into Dan Sullivan in Boise, Idaho. He introduced me to a friend of his from Montana, and I said, "I just wrote a song about Montana." Dan asked, "What's the story?" I told him the synopsis and he said, "That sounds like a novel."

Zach and Dan have been incredible through this process, helping turn a four-hundred-word song into an amazing novel. Without their dedication, direction, and insight, this book would have never been completed. Special thanks goes out to our incredible editor Beth, to Kim at Deranged Doctor for the cover design, to Coley McCabe-Shepherd and to Amy Sullivan for their support on this journey and journeys yet to be taken.

And thanks to all of you, our amazing friends and fans for the outpouring of love and support over the years.

Thom Shepherd
Christmas Eve 2018

CHAPTER ONE

He woke up that morning with a price on his head. The Lincoln Continental Jersey Boys wanted to see him dead. At age thirty-two, he thought he had it all: a beautiful wife, a thriving career, and over a million dollars tucked away in multiple investments. But now he had to figure out how to survive the day. If he made it through Tuesday, then he would lie awake all night worrying about how he was going to live through Wednesday.

By observation, most people would have incorrectly guessed that Charles Tinsley had grown up with money. He had an auspicious name and he dressed in expensive suits. The way he spoke and the way he carried himself all suggested that he came from a long line of wealth. But he had, in fact, grown up in a very middle-class Brooklyn family who struggled to make ends meet, barely able to send their three children to college.

His father, the owner of a Bushwick Avenue pharmacy, had worked long hours, keeping the little store open six, and then seven days a week as competition grew. The entire family worked in the little pharmacy. Charles started sweeping floors and running errands when he was six. His father urged his children to go to college and get a job. He encouraged them to get a career with a company that offered a decent living, a retirement plan, and normal working hours.

Charles attended Brooklyn College while living at home and working evenings and weekends at the pharmacy. He graduated with a C-plus average, earning him a degree in business with a minor in economics.

Charles Tinsley was destined for an entry level job at a large corporation. There he would likely spend his entire career frustrated in middle management positions until he retired with no hair and a tiny nest egg. His destiny changed when he ran into his Uncle Ed at a family gathering.

Ed Tinsley lived a much different life than his little brother. Ed was a stockbroker who seemed to do very well. He ran his business out of a little corner office in Jersey City, employing only his niece Monica as the receptionist. Uncle Ed had always driven a newer Cadillac. He lived in a modest home near Bergen Hill with his fifth wife, who Charles couldn't remember ever seeing sober or without a cigarette in her hand.

Short, overweight, and the king of the comb-over, Ed was the uncle who always sent Christmas cards to each niece and nephew containing twenty-dollar bills. When Charles told him about the interviews he had lined up, Ed said, "Those are bullshit positions for fucked-up companies. Why don't you come to work for me and make some real dough?"

Despite his parents' objections, four months later, Charles Tinsley was a Registered Financial Consultant with a new suit and a small box of business cards. He had a tiny desk in the corner of the little office, so close to his obnoxious cousin that he could turn and smack Monica in the back of the head every time she popped her gum.

The first hint that his uncle's business was anything other than what it appeared to be was on Charles' third day, when a small financial firm, kitty corner from the Saint Mary of the Immaculate Conception Church, came to lunch.

In the backroom of a little Italian café, Ed introduced him to the DiPiero brothers, his best clients. Charles was shocked to be sitting with celebrities of a sort. Everybody in

Jersey knew Frankie and Vince DiPiero, the heads of the notorious mob family. During the lunch, Ed introduced him to the brothers, telling them that Charles was his protégé, the young man that would run his business just as Ed had always operated it after he retired. The brothers looked at Charles with great suspicion, but he nodded and confirmed everything his uncle told them, even though he had no idea what it all meant.

On the way back to the office after lunch, Uncle Ed explained that he helped the DiPiero family move money between their various businesses. He guided and advised them on ways to convert the huge amounts of cash they acquired into solid investments.

Charles tried to twist his mind around the concept, then simply asked, "You launder money for the mob?"

Ed abruptly pulled the Cadillac to the curb. "Charlie, never use those words again. Not in this car, not in the office, not while floating by yourself in the middle of the fuckin' ocean. What you suggest is illegal. I might bend the rules, but I never break them," he lied. "You can have a good life and make a lot of money if you help the family and keep your mouth shut. Clear?"

Charles struggled with the morality of his new job. He thought about it every day until he received his first paycheck.

***

He didn't know what to do, he didn't know where to go, and he didn't know how to stop the brutal, perhaps even torturous death that was coming his way. The FBI had offered him their witness protection program, but he didn't think that would do anything but delay the inevitable. He was a dead man; he just didn't know when, or how, or how painful his death might be.

He needed to think. He needed to come up with a plan, but his head was so filled with fear, confusion, mixed emotions, and doubt that he felt cloudy, foggy, and unable to focus on anything. Jodi could tell there was something wrong, but she didn't pry too hard. She could tell he was agitated and nervous, but he told her everything was fine. He kissed her goodbye that morning, telling her not to answer the door for anybody.

"Why can't I answer the door?" his wife asked.

He thought up a quick lie. "The firm is involved in a bullshit lawsuit. They're going to try to serve me a subpoena, but I need to delay the court date a little longer while we dig up some old paperwork." He told her not to worry; the case would go away quickly once they found and presented the original contracts that protected them.

She bought it until a car on the street in front of their brownstone honked its horn. He jumped at the sound then raced to the window and peeked through the blinds. He looked up and down the street before racing down to the basement then out the backdoor.

She caught him at the bottom of the steps, stopping him before he got to the alley. "Chas, what the hell is going on?" She knew something bigger was going on in his life than just a worrisome lawsuit.

"I told you," he said. He had spent their entire marriage shielding her from the truth about his practice and his clients. He wasn't going to change that now.

"You told me something; now tell me the truth," she said, accusing him of lying for the first time ever.

"I'll tell you tonight," he said in an attempt to end the conversation.

She crossed her arms. "You need to tell me now. What's in the bag?" She pointed to the green duffle bag she had never seen before that hung from his shoulder.

"I don't have time to tell you now," he yelled out of both fear and frustration. She could see anger and fear in his eyes. "I've got to go, and you need to get back in the house and shut the damn door!"

"Get in here and talk to me!" she pleaded.

He turned and walked away without a word.

He walked the half block from their home to the parking garage with the duffle bag he had retrieved from the basement slung over his shoulder. At any moment, he expected a large man in an ill-fitted suit to step out from behind a corner to end his life. When he got to his car, he looked under it for anything unusual, then he opened the door and searched the interior but found nothing. He opened the hood while holding his breath; everything looked normal. It took him several seconds to build up the courage to start the engine, which fired on the first turn without the fireball he expected.

Leaving the garage, he turned right rather than the left turn he would normally take to get him to the Brooklyn-Queens Expressway. He drove north rather than south, watching his mirrors for any sign of a tail. He relied on everything he had learned from TV shows and movies over the years to help keep him alive for another day.

The junction of the Brooklyn-Queens Expressway and the Long Island Expressway happens to lie between the Calvary Cemetery and the First Calvary Cemetery, a place he and his friends had always referred to as "The Devil's Cloverleaf." As the expressway passed over the Calvary Cemetery, all he could think was "I'll see you all soon." His fate was inevitable. Avoiding it seemed futile and hopeless. He turned on Queens Boulevard toward the Queensboro Bridge and Midtown Manhattan.

***

Charles' rise from a Jersey City street corner broker to a Lower Manhattan equity trader in just ten years was nothing short of impressive. Uncle Ed retired a few years after Charles started working for him, turning his business and the management of the DiPiero family's funds over to him. The younger, more aggressive nephew took hold of the family's accounts and not only laundered their money, but found ways to rapidly grow their investment funds, gaining them huge returns.

Uncle Ed immediately moved to Boca Raton after divorcing wife number five. He bought a condo with a view of the beach, then two months later, died in his sleep. A rumor circulated that his death was suspicious; perhaps the family had tied up a loose end. Charles brushed it off. Uncle Ed's death was more likely caused by his diet, two packs a day, a lack of exercise, and a history of heavy drinking.

As the family's accounts grew, so did the monetary size of the portfolio that Charles managed. Soon he started receiving interest from larger financial institutions. Convinced that he could make greater returns with more tools, Charles accepted an offer, with approval from the DiPiero brothers, to work for the Clark Financial Group.

Clark Financial was a perfect fit. In a short period of time, they had grown from a small Queens-based firm to a real player on Wall Street. Like others, they had ridden the wave of a strong economy and weak financial regulations to grow from eight employees to over a hundred. Their practices skirted several laws, and their methods were questionable at best. They were in it for the money. They loved hiring guys like Tinsley.

Given the size of the financial portfolio Charles brought with him, he was able to bargain for his own assistant, a secretary, a company car with a parking space, and a window office on the 94th floor of the World Trade Center's North Tower.

His first order of business was to learn everything he could about the new penny stocks, the microcaps that were based around the fairly new internet. New companies sprang up every day, creating the opportunity for massive amounts of gains. The internet and email provided him with the opportunity to communicate with thousands of investors in minutes rather than the old method of picking up the phone and talking to only fifty to seventy-five a day.

His boss at Clark Financial thought he was crazy when he hired a geeky assistant, a recent college dropout named Ronny. But Charles knew it was a brilliant move. Ronny understood the internet and its capabilities. More than that, he understood the potential of this new instrument that most people still viewed as a toy.

With Ronny's help, he set up websites and email blasts. Ronny's wide network of techy friends fed him the names of startup dot-com businesses that had great potential with impressive business plans that promised massive growth and tremendous returns.

With his new tools and his new sources of information, Charles would pick a stock and invest a few million dollars of the family's money, sending the value of the penny stock through the roof. Then he would send out an email blast to a huge group of potential investors, telling them to look at the stock, which had recently risen a few hundred percent and was likely to continue rising.

Investors, seeing a three- or four-hundred-percent rise in an inexpensive stock over a two-day period would flock to it, sending the value even higher. When Charles saw a large increase in the value of the stock, he would dump the family's holdings and take the gains. Usually, the stock price would then tumble as everybody bailed out to save their original investments.

It was a brilliant plan that worked time after time. Unfortunately, the Securities and Exchange Commission, the SEC, referred to his strategy as a Pump and Dump scheme. Charles Tinsley soon appeared on their radar.

***

Traffic across the East River was always heavy, but as he neared the middle of the Queensboro Bridge, crossing Roosevelt Island, traffic ground to a halt. Ahead of him, some people were even getting out of their cars and looking downriver. Looking to his left, he saw a huge column of smoke rising from the World Trade Center. From his vantage point, he couldn't tell if the smoke came from the South Tower or from his building, the North Tower.

He flipped on the radio. "...reports coming in that an aircraft has hit the North Tower of the World Trade Center in Lower Manhattan. Smoke can be seen pouring out of the building..."

Concerns for his own life vanished as he got out of the car and gazed at the smoke rising against a perfect blue sky. He tried to call Ronny, but there was no answer. He tried to call the office's main line, but it just rang and rang. It didn't connect to voicemail as normal. He called Donna Bachleda, the office manager, then Becca, his secretary, but they didn't answer.

Charles returned to his car as traffic started to move again, then as he glanced back at the burning building, a second plane hit the South Tower. Charles suddenly felt like he was going to throw up.

He dialed Jodi to let her know he was okay, but he received a recorded message saying, "all circuits are busy" and to "please try your call later." His head spun. Jodi would think he had taken his normal route to work and that he was in his office by now. She would think he was still in the building.

No matter who he tried to call, he received the same message time and time again. Traffic moved at a painfully slow pace. By the time he got to the west side of the bridge, he had decided to turn onto Second Avenue and return across the bridge to Brooklyn. He was one of the last cars to make it onto the bridge as the police placed barriers, closing all Manhattan bridges to civilian traffic.

From the middle span of the bridge, he watched the South Tower collapse.

***

Just over a year before that horrible day, Special Agent Robert Anderst had first heard the name Charles Tinsley. Anderst had just taken over the ongoing FBI investigation into the DiPiero family. The last piece of advice Agent Katherine Huth had given him before her retirement was "Follow the money."

The money the DiPiero family had seemed to trace back, time after time, to Tinsley and the Clark Financial Group. But beyond that, Anderst couldn't find any signs of criminal activity in the hundreds of transactions he had investigated. Everything seemed to be above board, but he knew it wasn't.

Frustrated, he placed a call to a buddy over at the Securities and Exchange Commission to see if they had any information on Tinsley or Clark Financial. Within an hour, he received a call back from Investigator Joe Azevedo, who wanted to know why the FBI was investigating Tinsley and his firm.

"I'm investigating the DiPiero Family, and all the money seems to run back to Tinsley," Anderst told Azevedo.

Azevedo laughed. "I'm investigating Tinsley and trying to figure out where all the money comes from. How about you and I get together for lunch?"

Lunch that day consisted of a couple of hot dogs from a street vendor, washed down with two Cokes. It launched an eleven-month joint investigation that pointed to one common denominator, a man named Charles Tinsley.

CHAPTER TWO

It was probably a random event, but the sight of a black Lincoln Continental following him on an exit near his home spooked him. His own problems came crashing down on him again. He nearly hit a homeless man crossing the street as he turned left and gunned the engine. He sped through a yellow light and turned right, the opposite direction of his home, trying to lose the Lincoln. The radio reported the collapse of the North Tower. Charles pulled into an alleyway, turned off his engine, then cried for the first time since he was a child.

He couldn't go home to get Jodi for fear of his life and hers. He was under indictment by the FBI and the SEC. His career and his life as he knew them were over. His freedom was at stake, although he didn't believe he would live long enough to get to prison. If he did end up in prison, he would certainly die there. And now, in what was being reported as a suspected terrorist attack, he feared that many of his co-workers and friends might be dead.

The only way he could figure out how to keep his beautiful wife alive was to disappear. He figured that if they couldn't find him, they would keep an eye on her, hoping she would eventually lead them to him.

The commentary on the radio kept repeating itself, reporting what little they knew, speculating on the numbers that might have died. He started to call Jodi again to let her know he was okay, then realized that if she knew he was alive, her life would be in danger too. He set the phone on the seat next to him and tried to figure out his next move.

On the passenger seat next to his phone was his "go bag." The small green canvas duffle bag that he kept hidden in the basement had been a suggestion from his Uncle Ed. The bag contained a couple of new toothbrushes, his passport, two pair of underwear, and about twelve thousand dollars in small bills.

Uncle Ed had told him to prepare the bag and keep it where he could quickly get to it in case he ever had to leave suddenly. When Charles asked why he would need to leave, Ed brought up floods, earthquakes, an FBI investigation, or a falling out with the family.

As he listened to the reports on the radio, it occurred to him that if Jodi thought he was dead, maybe the FBI, the SEC, and the DiPiero family would believe it too. He needed to get out of town and disappear. He started the car and began making his way north.

***

The joint FBI/SEC investigation into Charles Tinsley and the DiPiero family yielded enough evidence to put Tinsley in prison for a very long time. But investigators and the attorney general's office still felt they lacked enough solid evidence to guarantee a conviction of the key members of the family.

In a conference room filled with special agents, investigators, prosecutors, and attorneys, the decision was made to confront Tinsley and see if they could cut a deal. Two days later, Special Agent Anderst walked into Tinsley's office, closed the door, pulled out his badge, and told the young man he was under arrest for securities fraud and manipulation.

Tinsley put up a strong front; he didn't look fazed at all. "You have no evidence to support your allegations," he told Anderst.

Anderst quietly opened his briefcase and began laying out stock valuation graphs, email blasts, and purchase and sale histories. By the time he was done, Tinsley had turned white.

"The attorney general tells me you're looking at forty years," said Anderst bluntly. "But there is a way to keep your butt out of prison. You might even be able to go home and sleep with your pretty wife tonight."

The attorney general's office had already sketched out a deal if Tinsley provided the documentation they needed to convict the DiPieros. If he provided the information along with something Anderst called a silent deposition, he wouldn't have to testify. The family would never know where the FBI acquired the evidence. Tinsley would lose his rights to ever work in the financial industry again, but he would serve no prison time.

He weighed his options for a several seconds. None of the alternatives he could think of stacked up to spending forty years behind bars. Tinsley took the deal.

Everything would have worked out if the DiPiero brothers had been as dumb as everyone thought. Becca, the trusted secretary that had worked for Charles for over a year, had a secret income. She made five hundred dollars cash each month to keep the family informed of anything unusual she noticed. It turned out to be money well spent.

***

Traffic out of the city was incredibly light as he drove north in the mid-morning sunshine. All the way to Hackensack, he saw fire engines, ambulances, and police cars racing the opposite direction, towards the chaos in Manhattan. A sense of patriotism seemed to be rising quickly. Two high-school-aged girls stood on an overpass waving a large American flag back and forth. He passed a motorhome. Somebody had used what appeared to be white shoe polish to write "God Bless America" on the back window in bold letters.

Once he was out of the city, away from the overloaded cell service around the disaster, his phone started to ring. He recognized all the numbers on the phone's display. Jodi tried to call again and again; he could only imagine the anguish she must be feeling. As he continued north, his mother tried to call him, then his brother, several friends, relatives, and finally, Vince DiPiero.

He drove, trying to figure out where to go and how to disappear in such a way that nobody would ever be able to find him. He needed to travel without leaving a trace. He couldn't get pulled over, and he couldn't use his phone, his credit cards, or his checkbook. He would have to find a job that paid him under the table, because he couldn't use his social security number or his real name again. Charles Tinsley had to completely and forever vanish.

Stopping at a gas station in Mifflinville, he filled his company car with fuel and paid with cash. He pulled his seldom-used gym bag out of the trunk, dumped out the contents, and dropped his cell phone, check book, passport, and credit cards inside. After adding a couple of rocks, he dropped it off the Market Street bridge into the Susquehanna River.

He drove four hours to Youngstown, Ohio before stopping to get a burger and gas. He was driving west, putting as much distance as he could between him and the DiPiero boys. He was driving away from everything he knew and everyone he loved.

Sitting in a McDonald's just off the freeway, he looked out at the silver BMW 5 Series that belonged to his company. He realized that it too had to disappear. If the car was found abandoned in the middle of Ohio, people back home might start to question how it came to be there and wonder if he'd really died in the North Tower. Authorities would expect to eventually find the remains of the car buried under a million tons of rubble in the parking garage, but he couldn't worry about that today. As he listened to the radio news reports covering the collapse of the towers, he acknowledged it could take months or even longer to clear the debris.

His mind spun. Thousands had died, according to the reports. He could have and probably should have been one of them. Jodi undoubtedly thought he was amongst the dead. He wanted so badly to call her, to send her an email, even a letter, something to let her know that he was still alive. Something to give her hope that she would see him again. But there was no way he could let her know, no way he could even send her a subtle hint that he was still alive somewhere. Doing so would endanger both of their lives.

***

After learning that the FBI and the SCE had been poking around Clark Financial, the DiPiero brothers had started their own investigation. They hired a private investigator named John Frinzi. Frinzi's job was to find out what the FBI knew and what, if anything, Tinsley might have told them.

Frinzi, a retired federal marshal, called an old buddy at the FBI. It took Frinzi so little time and effort to get the information the DiPieros had asked for that he waited two full days to meet with them and go over his findings.

What he told the brothers caused Frankie's ulcer to immediately act up. He clutched his stomach. Vince just became angry. By the end of the day, Charles Tinsley was as good as a dead man. Vince was going to kill the young man himself, but Frankie insisted they send Jimmy White after him. It was a delicate matter. There could never be any evidence that indicated Tinsley had been murdered, and his body could never be found. Vince had been anything but subtle in the past. The last thing they needed was the guy's bloody body to be found in a Jersey dumpster.

Jimmy White had done work for them in the past. He was a true professional. When asked, he could make people disappear forever. White had never been arrested; he hadn't even had a speeding ticket in nearly forty years. The police didn't know the guy existed because he had never come up on their radar.

White was expensive but worth every penny. He accepted the job and said he would report back when it was complete. He didn't expect payment until the job was finished and the client was satisfied.

Becca Locklear, Tinsley's secretary, wasn't a professional. Vince DiPiero's mistake was telling her that Tinsley was a dead man for talking to the FBI. Feeling guilty and responsible, she left an anonymous typewritten note under the wiper blade on his car, warning him of the death threat from DiPiero.

***

Charles arrived in the outskirts of Chicago just before midnight. He was dead-tired after a crazy, emotion-filled day. After a brief search, he located a little motel in a dilapidated Calumet City neighborhood and paid $49.00 for a clean but well-used room. Filling out the registration form, Charles used the name Steven Smith and a made-up address in Kansas City. He was asleep five minutes after his head hit the pillow.

The following morning was beautiful and sunny, but he couldn't stomach turning on the news. He couldn't bear to hear the reports that detailed the numbers dead. Charles didn't want to think about the hundreds of people he saw in the building every day, many of them now dead or hopelessly buried in the debris.

Instead, he turned his thoughts to his own survival. The lady at the front desk gave him directions to a Target store, where he bought a small wardrobe of inexpensive jeans, shoes, tee-shirts, a hooded sweatshirt, and a winter jacket.

Then he drove north towards the city until he found the right kind of neighborhood.

Charles had grown up in a fiercely Catholic, Republican, law-abiding family who lived in a conservative park of Brooklyn. But a few blocks from his neighborhood, the streets were tougher. He went to high school with car thieves, drug dealers, pimps, hookers, thugs, and a host of other interesting characters. The education Charles received in his high school classrooms wasn't nearly as interesting as the lessons he learned in the hallways and alleys after school.

Relying on his alternate education, he parked in front of a chain-link fenced autobody shop on a side street off Damen Avenue. Dressed in jeans and a tee-shirt, he walked in and asked to speak to the owner.

"What can I do for ya?" asked the man behind the desk.

"I've got a car I need to get rid of," he answered.

"I don't buy cars," said the man with a bit of a growl. "Leo Potts, two blocks down the street. Go see him."

"I didn't say I wanted to sell it," replied Charles.

The man looked up and studied him for a moment. "You a cop?"

"I ain't no cop. I got a new Beamer. It needs to go away forever…but if you're not interested."

The man stood up, "Well, I can at least have a look. Maybe I can point you in the right direction."

As they walked out to the street, the shop owner asked, "Do you own it?"

"No," said Charles.

"So it's stolen?"

"Not really. The company that owned it no longer exists."

The owner pointed to the New York license plates. "You're not wound up in that mess at the World Trade Center, are you? You're not some terrorist?"

"I didn't have anything to do with that," Charles replied quietly.

"So what do you want to do with this?" asked the man.

"I need it to go away. I need it to vanish," said Charles. "I know there's chop shops around that can make it all go away. I need the V.I.N. numbers to disappear and the license plates cut into little pieces."

The man knew the parts that could be easily harvested from the BMW were easily worth more than fifteen grand. "What do you need out of the deal?" he asked.

"Something reliable," said Charles.

The owner pointed to an older rusty Ford pickup that sat just inside the fence. "That's my truck. She doesn't look very pretty, but mechanically, she's solid. I'd drive her anywhere."

Charles glanced at the truck, nodded, then they exchanged keys. "That car has to disappear."

"By this time tomorrow, it won't exist," said the man with a smile.

***

Jimmy White rarely saw this side of his work. Sitting in his car, across the street and down the block from the Tinsley brownstone, he watched as friends and family came and went. A woman he believed to be Jodi Tinsley came out of her home a time or two. She looked distraught and tired. Her hair was a mess, her face was white, her expression was blank.

Each group that came brought food. As he imagined the hams, casseroles, and Jell-O salads accumulating inside the home, his stomach growled. The guests consoled each other as they left the house. An older woman was so overcome with grief as she left the house that she had to be aided by a younger man. They were certainly acting like Tinsley was dead.

A uniformed police officer double-parked then knocked on the door. He spoke to the distraught woman for a few minutes then left. A priest arrived and went into the home for about a half hour before leaving. Two guys in cheap suits and a government-issued sedan slowly drove by a couple of times, probably the FBI.

Jimmy was glad he wouldn't have to be the one to kill Tinsley. He seemed to have a nice family.

***

The dark blue 1974 Ford F-100 started with a puff of oily exhaust on the first turn. Charles was relieved that it was an automatic because he'd never driven a manual transmission. She was perfect, a nearly invisible vehicle. She was an old pickup, a work truck. She was the type of vehicle that nobody paid any attention to; nobody took a second look. Both lower rocker panels were rusted and nearly gone. The bed was dented from use; several small car parts lay back there. The interior was dirty, and it smelled of oil and gas. The vinyl on the seat was torn. A blanket sort of covered the hole.

He drove her a few blocks before stopping to fill the tank and check the oil. He checked to make sure the lights and blinkers worked. He couldn't get pulled over for any reason. He paid for his gas with cash and purchased a U.S. map.

Laying the map across the hood of the old truck, he decided to drive north to Minneapolis then west into North Dakota. He needed to find a place where he would be so lost that the FBI, the SEC, and the DiPiero Brothers would never be able to find him. He needed to become a ghost.

Driving north on I-90, he quickly learned that his new truck wasn't a BMW. Her steering was loose, and she liked to wander across the highway. At anything over sixty miles an hour, she was a bit scary. Everything rattled. He cracked the window to help alleviate the exhaust fumes that entered the cab. And she drank a lot of fuel. He limped into Mauston, Wisconsin on empty.

***

Jimmy White sat across the table from the brothers in a coffee shop a few blocks south of the turnpike. "I think your man's dead."

"Yeah?" said Vince DiPiero. "How do we know for sure?"

"You may never know for sure," replied White. "The jet fuel in that plane burned so hot that they'll probably never find his body."

Frankie leaned forward. "How do we know he was in his office when the plane hit?"

"All I can tell you is this," said White. "His wife and his mother think he's dead. I've seen their faces."

"We need to be sure. This guy can't surface somewhere in a witness protection program and testify against us," said Vince.

Jimmy White smiled calmly. "Okay, you tell me how we can be sure."

Frankie raised his hand, stopping his brother's coming tirade. Vince closed his mouth. The brothers' unique and different personalities worked together well. Frankie was the older brother. He had the business savvy, while his younger brother, Vince, had the muscles, and he wasn't afraid to use them. "Is it possible he got out of the building and is hiding somewhere?" asked Frankie calmly.

"Anything's possible," said White matter-of-factly. "He had to know that you would eventually find out about the FBI investigation. Maybe he or the FBI took the opportunity to have him play dead. But as of yesterday afternoon, his family didn't think he was alive. I'm sure of that."

"We gotta fuckin' know for sure," said Vince.

"I understand," said White. He didn't know what he was supposed to do about it, but he understood their concerns.

***

The day after the terrorist attack on the World Trade Center, all the resources of the FBI in New York City were diverted away from non-critical cases. Special Agent Robert Anderst stuffed the contents of the DiPiero case into a file. Recalling his recent visit to Tinsley's 94th floor office, he placed a call to the New York City Police Department, asking them to do a welfare check on Tinsley. They reported back a few hours later that, according to his wife, he was among the missing. Local newscasters were reporting that American Airlines Flight 11 hit the North Tower between the 93rd and 99th floors. He made a note on the file and locked it in his filing cabinet for the future.

Anderst wished he could somehow make the events of September 11th go away and get back to his mundane job chasing mob bosses and crooked stock brokers.

CHAPTER THREE

After fueling and getting a bite to eat in Mauston, Charles took I-94 towards Minneapolis. It never occurred to him that Minneapolis might have a rush hour. It wasn't something he had ever considered, but he had never been there. The city was bigger than he would have guessed. He realized there was a lot he didn't know about his country.

The Tinsley family had never taken a real vacation. Because of the drugstore, the longest vacations they had ever taken were a few overnight trips to Coney Island or down the Shore.

He and Jodi had taken a few trips. They honeymooned in Jamaica and had taken a trip to Florida, but always by airplane. He had never driven this far in his life, and he had never been this far west.

It was dark by the time he got out of Minneapolis. He kept driving until he was simply too tired to go any further. He pulled off and found a room at the Gopher Prairie Inn in Salk Centre, Minnesota. On the room registration, he made up a name and an address in Denver.

After checking in, he went to the room and dropped his green duffle bag and the brown duffle he had bought at Target onto the bed. The guy at the front desk told him there was a bar with decent food just across the main road. He walked a block over to a restaurant/bar combination called Elmerz, where he found a seat at the bar and ordered a Bud draft.

"Is the kitchen still open?" he asked the bartender.

"He's cleaning up back there, but we might be able to find you something. Let me go ask him."

The short, squatty bartender with a bad hip returned with a plate containing a couple of pieces of fried chicken and some French fries. "This is all he had back there, but you can have it if you want. He was just about to throw it out."

The cold chicken and fries tasted wonderful. He washed them down with a beer and then another. He hadn't realized how hungry he was.

"Wow," said the bartender. "You devoured that!" He took the plate away and returned with a third beer. "Just passing through?"

"Yeah, I'm on my way up to North Dakota to do a little hunting," he lied.

"I hear the pheasant are thick this year. I'm Rick," he said while stretching to extend his arm across the bar.

"I'm...Will," he said, spotting a Will Rogers quote hanging above the bar. He couldn't remember if Will Rogers or Roy Rogers was the singer his father liked, but he decided at that moment to start using the name Will Roy. The name sounded like a cowboy from North Dakota rather than a Manhattan securities dealer.

Charles Tinsley was dead. Will Roy was a guy in jeans and a tee-shirt who hadn't shaved in two days. He was just an ordinary dude driving an old truck towards North Dakota, drinking Budweiser in a bar off the interstate, chatting it up with the bartender.

***

Everything in Jodi's world had turned upside down. She couldn't eat, she couldn't sleep, and she couldn't think. She couldn't even remember what trivial thing they argued about at the backdoor as he left. She could only remember that her last words to him were filled with anger, not love. She remembered that he had raised his voice at her. The last time she saw his face, he was yelling at her in frustration and rage.

He was always in the office at least an hour before the markets opened. Based on the time he left the house, he would have easily been in his office when the plane hit the building. If he had been late, if for some reason he hadn't made it to the office in time, she would have heard from him by now.

Her mother had finally arrived from Syracuse and was able to answer the seemingly endless phone calls and shield her from the line of well-intentioned people who showed up unannounced at her door. She should have appreciated everybody's concerns, and she knew she probably would later, but right now, she was dealing with her own demons.

Jodi had met Charles in a bar. He had introduced himself to her after they made eye contact. Their first formal date didn't go very well; it was awkward and uncomfortable. For some reason, she agreed to a second date with him. At that dinner, the conversation flowed, they laughed, and she found herself captivated by the charming young financial advisor. Four months later, he proposed to her. She said, "Maybe." It took her two months to accept his proposal and his elegant ring. It wasn't that she was uncertain about him; she was unsure of her own insecurities and fears.

After four years of marriage, they still hadn't decided on children. Charles' career was demanding, he left for work early and came home exhausted. His recent move to Clark Financial Group gave him a secretary and an assistant, which he had hoped would increase his income while reducing the time and effort he spent at work. So far, it hadn't. He seemed to be working harder and longer hours.

Her job as a paralegal for a Brooklyn law firm was demanding as well. The group of attorneys she worked for were involved in a huge water-rights lawsuit that would likely stretch on for decades. At home, Charles and Jodi worked extra hours, but as a rule, Sundays were sacred. They spent the entire day together. They might spend the day doing laundry or grocery shopping, but they always spent the whole day with each other, and any kind of job-related work was prohibited.

After spending more than an hour in the dark, staring out their bedroom window at a distant street light, her mother came into the room with a bowl of soup. "You need to eat this," she said.

"I will," said Jodi quietly.

"I'll just sit here while you eat," said her mom, seeing through Jodi's weak promise.

Jodi looked at her mom, her eyes hollow. "I don't know what to do. I don't know what I should be doing."

Rozella Hopkins didn't know what to tell her daughter. She had never experienced anything like this either. But she knew she couldn't be indecisive or uncertain. She needed to be Jodi's rock. "Eat your soup, then let's have a look at your finances. We'll make sure all your bills are current and then start planning for October."

Jodi shook her head with a slight smile. Her mother was such a realist. Jodi would hold out hope for years that Charles was out there somewhere, unconscious in a hospital or buried alive in a small but comfortable space under the rubble, just waiting to be found. Her mother was already planning for the worst-case scenario. Jodi refused to consider he wasn't alive, but looking at the bills was something she could do to help take her mind off everything else.

After eating her soup, they moved to the den, where she logged on to their Chase bank account. "Good Lord, Jodi," said her mother. "Where in the world did you get all that money?"

The checking account showed just over seventy-five thousand dollars. Their investment accounts showed another eight hundred thousand dollars. She knew Charles also had accounts with a few other investment firms. She didn't answer the question. She was busy trying to decipher the strange information on the screen.

"Why does the balance show those amounts," asked her mother, "but the available balance shows as zero on all the accounts?"

Jodi looked at the discrepancy. "I have no idea. That's strange. I'll call them in the morning."

***

Damon Wilkes had never had an easy life. He grew up in Washington Park, near the railroad yard, south of Chicago. He spent time in and out of foster homes and juvenile detention centers for minor crimes. He didn't think he was a bad person; he simply considered himself unlucky. He had friends who seemed to get away with anything. If he spit on the sidewalk, his spit always seemed to land on the shoe of some racist white cop.

He had done less and gotten busted more than anybody he knew. But at twenty-three, he was trying to get straight and work hard. He was done hanging out with the gangs, and he was done trying to make easy money. He got a job at an auto body shop on the southside and was working hard to learn a trade. The old man who owned the shop was a grump, but he was also patient with Damon, teaching him the business. Before long, the young man started doing some projects on his own. He loved seeing a crumpled fender look new again. He felt he had a knack for it. He was proud of his work.

It was an honor when the old man asked him to drive the shiny new BMW he had bought over to JP's Automotive. He loved the look and the feel of the car. He wished he could have driven it where some of his friends could have seen him. The owner had been specific. Take the car to JP's, remove the license plates, bring them back here, and cut the plates into a hundred pieces with the plasma cutter. Until he arrived at JP's in Englewood, he had no idea what he had been asked to do. It didn't take him more than a few seconds to know that the car was heading for a chop shop. In a matter of hours, it would be dismantled, and the parts would be sold. He removed the plates as he was instructed then took a cab back to his own shop.

It seemed a shame to cut the New York license plates into little pieces. He decided instead to keep them and put them up on the wall of the little room he rented a few blocks from the shop. He had always wanted to see New York. Maybe the plates would give him the motivation to save some money for a future trip.

***

Charles slept fitfully, waking from a nightmare. In his dream, he watched an airliner hit his office. He ran through the flames trying to save his co-workers, but when he tried to help them from the floor, their badly burnt arms pulled from their shoulders. Ronny, lying armless on the floor, asked him, "Why did you leave us?"

He woke in a sweat then lay in the bed thinking of the hell Jodi must be going through. He had heard that everybody above the 93rd floor likely died. His 94th floor office faced east, and the plane had hit the north side of the building. Jodi had to believe that he had died instantly. He wanted so badly to call her, to tell her he was okay. But he knew that would likely put her life at risk. The brothers wouldn't touch her as long as they were convinced that he was dead. The moment she quit playing the part of widow, they would grab her and probably torture her until she gave up his location.

By 4:30am, he had enough. He got up and decided to drive towards North Dakota. If he got tired, he could sleep along the way, but he couldn't lie in that bed any longer. He couldn't spend any more time alone with his thoughts.

The sun was just starting to rise as he pulled into Fargo. He was hungry and out of gas. Taking the 45th Street exit, he turned north and found an IHOP. It wasn't the local Ma and Pa restaurant he had hoped to find, but he was famished.

The hostess, Mindy, sat him at a booth across from another man who was sitting alone. Charles thought he looked like a trucker or a farmer based on the way he was dressed. They nodded at each other.

"Which way ya headed?" asked the man across the aisle.

"West," said Charles.

"How far west?" he asked.

Charles didn't want anybody to know where he was going, even a stranger in a booth. "I don't know. I guess until I find a place I like, or until my truck breaks down."

"Ya ever driven across North Dakota before?" he asked.

"Nope. I'm looking forward to it." Charles replied.

"Gawd." The man laughed. "Don't stop until you get a hundred miles across the Montana border. That's some of the most awful country the good Lord ever made."

Charles took the opportunity to get more information out of the older man. "I'd like to get a job, maybe on a farm or a ranch. Is North Dakota a good place to look?"

The man scoffed at his comment. "There's plenty of ranches out there, but take it from me, go to Montana. North Dakota has some of the most brutal winters in the entire U.S. There ain't a tree or a mountain out there to stop the wind. It's every bit as cold in Montana, but the wind don't blow fifty miles an hour every day."

"I guess you're not with the North Dakota Chamber of Commerce?" said Charles with a chuckle.

The man shook his head and smiled. "No, I spent my share of winters out there. I guess I'm a bit jaded by my frost-bit toes." He finished his coffee, picked up his bill, and stood up. "Good luck to you," he said as he walked towards the cashier.

After a big breakfast, Charles stopped at an auto parts store, where he bought a case of oil. The truck was burning about a quart per tank of gas and the gas stations charged a premium for their oil. He turned west on I-94, and fifteen minutes later, he was out of town driving in a world he had never imagined existed.

Charles knew from watching westerns and other movies that the country had once been vast with large, wide-open spaces. He didn't know those spaces still existed, not like this. His windshield was full of immense emptiness. Growing up in New York, he had never seen so much vacant space in his entire life. It was, at the same time, amazingly beautiful and a bit frightening.

He passed a singlewide trailer that sat a few hundred yards off the interstate. He looked around and figured their closest neighbor was at least two miles away. At his Brooklyn brownstone, his closest neighbor was on the other side of the wall. He guessed that a hundred thousand people, maybe more, lived within two miles of his home. Looking around at the emptiness, he said to himself, "Population explosion, my ass."

***

Jodi woke from a dreamless night into the conscious world, which was its own nightmare. As she woke from an innocent night's sleep, all the details of the last three days came back, seemingly trying to crush her. Her mother was awake and sitting over a cup of coffee making a list of tasks they needed to complete. Rozella was sure that keeping busy was healthier than sitting around in a dark home, stewing over the unknown and dwelling in pity.

After a cup of coffee, Jodi logged in to their bank accounts again. The available balances still showed as zero. She called the 800 number and eventually reached a customer service representative who was only able to tell her that the accounts had some type of hold on them. Jodi asked if all the 9/11 victims had such holds on their accounts, but the person on the other end of the line didn't know.

"They don't know why the accounts have holds on them," said Jodi as she re-joined her mother at the kitchen table. "I'll go down to the bank when they open." Her mother jotted that on the growing list.

***

It was a beautiful, sunny morning. What the man at the IHOP had told him about the terrain was true. He was fascinated by the millions of empty, flat acres that stretched out on all sides of him. Hitting the peak of a slight rise—it couldn't even be considered a hill—he thought he could see the curvature of the earth on the flat horizon to the west. He spotted a herd of either deer or antelope, he wasn't sure which they were, standing not more than a hundred yards off the freeway. Other than the zoo, he had never seen a wild animal larger than a squirrel or a rat.

Out of boredom, he turned on the truck's AM radio and searched for a station. It reminded him of his father's old Chrysler. The stock push-button radio gave the driver the ability to store their five favorite stations. A single speaker was mounted in the middle of the dash. On a perfect day, parked next to the station's antenna, the quality of the sound was bad. Finally finding a country station out of Minneapolis, he heard almost as much static as music.

He wasn't a country music fan, but it was the only station he could pick up. All the songs they played seemed to have patriotic undertones. Lee Greenwood's song, "God Bless the USA," played every third or fourth tune. Charlie Daniel's "In America" played a couple of times. Then a new song by David Ball caught his attention, "Riding with Private Malone." It was about a man just out of the service who found a great deal on a Corvette. In the glovebox, he discovered a note from the original owner, Andrew Malone. It said he was going off to Vietnam and "If you're reading this, I didn't make it home." Charles listened intently. The song told about the kid getting into a fiery crash one night, and witnesses saw an unidentified soldier pull him out of the car. Nobody knew who that soldier was, but he always would know that it was Private Malone. It was an interesting ghost story that he wanted to hear again.

Charles knew he was a ghost. A man who had died in the inferno caused by a plane smashing into his building, or the resulting collapse of the tower. He hoped, for Jodi's sake, that the DiPiero brothers, the FBI, and his life insurance company all believed the same thing.

Pulling into Bismarck on fumes, he reminded himself not to stretch it so far. Running out of gas on the freeway might cause a state trooper to stop to help. It seemed likely they might ask to see his driver's license and question why the truck wasn't registered in his name. He couldn't risk any interaction with law enforcement. He was a felon on the run.

His biggest fear was being discovered alive by the DiPiero family. As he pumped gas into his truck, he felt safe. He was so far from New Jersey that it didn't seem possible the brothers would ever find him. Every mile he drove west was another mile of security. The mountains of Montana seemed even safer. The mountains seemed like they would shield and protect him. There he could hide in their canyons; he could slip away in the thousands of acres of timber that he had only seen in pictures.

He started to believe that he had slipped through the cracks and might survive.

CHAPTER FOUR

Mike Patterson, the manager of the Chase Bank branch on 7th Avenue, had known Charles and Jodi Tinsley for several years. They were good clients who carried large balances with his branch. When he watched the news coverage of the 9/11 attacks, he worried, knowing that Charles Tinsley's office was in one of the buildings. When Jodi walked in that morning, he could tell by the look on her face that the news wasn't good.

He jumped up and escorted her and her mother to the chairs at his desk. He wanted to ask about Charles but feared the worst.

"What can I help you with?" he asked.

Jodi removed her sunglasses. Her eyes were bloodshot and dull. "Something is strange with our accounts. They all show the correct balances, but all of the available balances are zero."

"Let's have a look," said Patterson. He pulled up her accounts and did some clicking around within the account before picking up the phone. "I'll call branch support and see what I can find out."

After a few minutes on the phone, using a lot of terms that Jodi didn't understand, he hung up and cleared this throat. "It seems that your accounts have been frozen by a court order."

"Are they doing that to all the Trade Center victims?" she asked.

"No," said Patterson. "Your accounts were frozen on Monday, the tenth. It seems there is some type of investigation being conducted. A federal court order was delivered to us three days ago." Looking at her face, he asked, "You don't know anything about this?"

She truthfully answered that she didn't.

"Who do we speak with about this?" asked Jodi's mother.

"I'd start with your attorney," he replied.

***

Three hours and one gas stop later, Charles crossed the Montana State line. He couldn't say he was impressed. He'd expected more, but then remembered that the man at breakfast had told him not to stop until he was a hundred miles inside the state. At Glendive, the freeway started following the Yellowstone River, which was beautiful when he could see it through the foliage that grew on its banks. At Custer, everything started changing. The freeway began to wander through rolling hills, trees started appearing on the landscape. Every mile became a little more interesting.

By the time he reached Billings, he was spent. He pulled off, fueled up his truck at the Conoco, then drove into town, turning right onto Main Street. A little more than a mile up Main, he spotted the Twin Cubs Motel, a 1950s/60s era motel that looked inexpensive. He rented a room for thirty-nine dollars for the night then took the clerk's suggestion and walked across the street to the Eagles Club for a bite to eat.

The local Fraternal Order of Eagles Club was the happening place in town on a Friday night. Or, at least it was a happening place for the over-sixty crowd. Karaoke was just starting when Charles arrived. He ordered a burger and a beer. An older gentleman sang "Achy Breaky Heart" before two middle-aged ladies, who the DJ announced as the Kendrick twins, sang a questionable version of "I Got You, Babe."

The nice couple sitting next to him started chatting with him. He found it a little easier each time to make up his back story. He told them he was from a little town south of Chicago. He was on his way to Missoula to help his uncle, who was suffering from gout. When they asked his uncle's name, because they knew a lot of people out that way, he made up Ed Roy, a combination of his late Uncle Ed's first name and his newly adopted last name. The couple didn't think they knew Ed Roy but said they'd pray for him and the serious case of gout he was suffering.

"Ginger root," said the lady next to him. "Put a little bit of ginger root into everything you cook for him and have him eat a small piece of ginger root daily. It will clear up his gout in no time," she assured him.

Charles finished his burger and washed it down with the beer. He got a hug and a kiss from the nice lady and shook the man's hand before walking back to his room. It was cold out, a different cold than he was used to, reminding him that he had left his coat in the truck.

In the visitor's guide he found in his room, he read that the town of Billings sat at an elevation of 3,123 feet above sea level. He had grown up and lived at sea level his entire life. Besides a few airline trips, he figured this was the highest he had ever been. Looking at the map he spread out on the bed, he could see that tomorrow the road would even climb higher. He was heading towards the Rocky Mountains. A strange twinge of excitement welled up inside of him.

***

Mac Telford returned to his office late after a very long day in court and dinner with a prospective client. In the middle of his desk was a big note from his secretary with Jodi's name and number. It said, "Call ASAP."

"Jodi, I'm so sorry to hear about Charles. Is there any word?" the attorney asked when she answered the phone.

"No," said Jodi. "We're just praying and hoping like everybody else," she replied. "It's been really hard."

"I'm so sorry you're going through this. Evelyn and I are praying for you and Charles. How else can I help you?" asked Telford.

Mac had known the couple for several years. Once a year, he invited each of his best clients out to dinner, and every year, he and his wife hosted a big Christmas party in their spacious Midtown apartment. He felt like he knew the young couple fairly well, so he was shocked when Charles had called him and told him about the issues with the SEC and the FBI. Mac asked Charles to tell him everything, to be sure not to leave out any detail. He was surprised by the confessions of the bright young man. The depth of his troubles seemed to have no end.

"Our bank accounts are frozen. The bank said it was something to do with a federal court order. Do you know anything about that?" asked Jodi.

Mac was a bit shocked that she didn't know about her husband's business dealings. He felt awkward being the one to tell her about the legal problems her husband, possibly her late husband, had gotten himself into. He let out a big sigh. "Do you have time for breakfast tomorrow?"

Jodi, hearing his sigh and his tone, was suddenly worried. "What's going on? Can my mother and I come to your office now?"

Mac shook he head. "If it's okay with you, I'll drop by your house on my way home." He hung up the phone and started to organize his thoughts. How was he going to explain to her the shit storm of legal trouble her husband had created?

As Charles was crawling into his bed at the modest Twin Cubs Motel off Main Street in Billings, Mac Telford was violating every aspect of attorney-client privilege by telling Jodi and her mother, Rozella, everything he knew about the man's legal issues.

The two women sat and patiently listened as Mac used a lot of legal jargon to explain the situation. Finally, Jodi's mother interrupted him. "What does all this mean in layman's terms?"

Mac looked up at the ceiling for a moment before answering. "Charles took over his Uncle Ed's firm. Uncle Ed had been laundering money for a mob family for years."

Rozella threw herself back in her chair, saying, "Oh, good grief."

Mac continued. "In the past couple of years, Charles started using some illegal methods to make huge sums of money for his clients, including the mob. It sounds like the Securities and Exchange Commission caught on to his schemes about the same time that the FBI figured out who was laundering the mob's money. In an attempt to keep his butt out of jail, he agreed to testify against the mob family."

Jodi couldn't believe what the man was telling them about her husband. It sounded like something out of a movie and nothing like the kind, gentle, hardworking man she knew. "Which family?" she quietly asked.

Mac cleared his throat. "The DiPiero family," he replied. He looked her in the eyes. "You really didn't know about any of this?"

Jodi shook her head.

"Is my daughter in danger or in any legal trouble?" asked Rozella.

"That's a very good question," replied Mac. "I don't believe there are currently any legal allegations against her, but I'll ask the district attorney that question in the morning. If the accusations are upheld, they will likely seize your assets, sell everything off, and use the funds to provide restitution to those who lost money due to the schemes."

"What about the mob?" asked Rozella. "You said Charles had agreed to testify against them. Will they try to hurt Jodi?"

Mac shrugged his shoulders. "That's not my area of expertise. I don't know if the DiPiero family knows that Charles was working with the FBI, the SEC, and the district attorney's office." He treaded lightly on the next subject. "If Charles is not available to testify, the documentation that he turned over may or may not be enough to bring indictments against them. If they do continue with the case without his testimony, the family would gain nothing by harming Jodi."

"But she will lose her house, her car, and everything in the bank accounts?" asked Rozella.

Mac grimaced. "Based on the evidence that I've seen, and the statements that Charles made to the SEC, yes. It will all be used to pay restitution to the victims."

None of it mattered to Jodi. She sat in a deepening stupor as she listened to the attorney talk about a man she thought she knew. A man she thought had high morals and integrity, a man she slept next to every night, who talked about children and their future. She felt cheated, deflated, and alone.

***

Charles woke feeling exhilarated. He spread his map open on the bed and looked at his options. He was tired of driving freeways and interstates. He wanted to slow down and see some of the countryside. After picking a route, he stopped by McDonalds for breakfast, something he swore he would never do again. With his sausage-egg sandwich and a large coffee, he drove across Wicks Lane to where it intersected with Alkali Creek Road and turned north. A few miles later, he turned onto Highway 3, which, if he took the correct turns, would lead him to Helena. He knew nothing about the town of Helena, but it sounded like a peaceful place, free of mobsters and FBI agents.

As he drove up the two-lane road, he looked at the occasional ranches he passed. He marveled at the number of American flags he noticed flying. They flew from mailboxes, front porches, and barns. Somebody had lined almost a half mile of the highway with small flags, one on each fence post on both sides of the road. He started seeing flags flying from the back of pickup trucks, and one creatively hung from a power line that crossed the road as he entered the little town of Comanche.

After passing through Comanche, he drove through Lavina, where he turned onto Highway 12, which followed the Musselshell River. It was a mere creek compared to the East and the Hudson Rivers that he was used to seeing. It was far more scenic than the New York rivers as it meandered slowly alongside the road. He drove thinking to himself that he had never seen so many cattle or so much barbed wire in his life.

Wandering along the two-lane highway, he felt a strange emotion well up inside of him. Perhaps it was some primal instinct, something hidden deep inside of him from generations of men before him. He felt like he belonged out here. He felt strangely comfortable in jeans and an old pickup, driving past cattle ranches on a remote road. He rolled down the window, put his elbow up on the door, and slowed down a bit to enjoy the scenery. He waved at other trucks as they met on the highway. He watched the drivers of the other trucks wave with just the fingers of their hand as it lay atop the steering wheel. He emulated the local practice.

***

No matter how Rozella sliced and diced the numbers, her daughter's financial situation looked bleak. Her job as a paralegal didn't bring in enough to make the house payment and utilities. Luckily, they didn't have any debt besides a few small balances on credit cards from the previous month.

She was sitting at the kitchen table with bills and other papers scattered around, when Jodi walked in. "Good morning, dear. Did you get any sleep?"

Jodi, dressed in a baggy tee-shirt and pajama pants, walked straight to the coffee pot and poured herself a cup. "Not a wink."

Rozella shook her head. "I think I have it all worked out. The Feds are going to take the house anyway, so why make any more payments? Your car has a little value to it, so let's sell it and you can ride the bus to work. That takes care of parking and insurance payments."

Jodi gave her mother a tired look. "Can we discuss this later? I'm really not in the mood."

"Well, I just thought if we could..."

Jodi cut her off. "I appreciate what you're trying to do, but now is not the right time."

Rozella got the message. "How much time can you take off work?" she asked.

"My boss said to take all the time I needed," she replied quietly. "I don't know how long I can stretch that."

"I wonder if we should go to Syracuse for a while, just to make sure this DiPiero family doesn't try anything."

Jodi looked at the ground. "I can't leave until I know if he's alive or..."

Rozella stood and hugged her daughter. "I know you can't, dear. I know you can't."

***

He arrived in Helena mid-afternoon. At the gas station, he bought a Montana state map and asked for directions to a local thrift shop. At the Goodwill store, for under a hundred dollars, he found a pair of cowboy boots and a hat, both used and nicely worn. He found some used jeans, a couple of shirts, and a light brown Carhart jacket that fit him well. He walked back out to his truck looking and feeling like a real cowboy.

Charles drove around town for a bit until he found the Overland Express Bar and Restaurant on 11th Avenue. He bellied up to the bar and ordered a beer. Martinis had been his drink of choice the last several years, but there was something about a tall, cold beer that seemed fitting. Sitting in a tavern like the Overland Express wearing a cowboy hat and boots and ordering a martini seemed completely inappropriate.

The man sitting at the bar next to him wore a golf shirt but also wore jeans and boots. "How ya doing?" he asked Charles.

"Hey, it's Saturday afternoon. I've got a cold beer in front of me and enough money in my pocket for another. I'm doing great," replied Charles with a smile.

They struck up a conversation about the weather, then about the September 11th attacks. The man next to him was very opinionated about what we should do in retaliation, once we figured out who was responsible. When asked, Charles told him he was from a little farming community in Illinois. He told the man he was looking for a job. What kind of job and where didn't really matter all that much, maybe something up in the mountains.

Charles knew he needed a job where he could work under the table, a job that would pay him in cash. As a fugitive, he would never again be able to work a job where his employer reported his social security number to the IRS. His friends at the FBI and the SEC would surely be watching for that. The DiPiero brothers had likely hired somebody to watch for him to reappear in some computer data base too.

"If you got nothing holding you back, and you like the mountains, I'd head for the Flathead Valley. That's some of the prettiest country in the entire world up there," said the man.

"Where's that?" he asked.

"Northwest of here, up towards Kalispell. Everything from there to the Canadian border is God's country."

The man described the valley and the mountains to him with a smile. He obviously loved the area. After hearing the man's description of the Flathead Valley, something seemed to call him there. He felt drawn to a place that he had never heard of before.

***

Jimmy White looked across the table, over the top of his cocktail at the very serious-looking DiPiero brothers. "I haven't been able to determine anything yet," he explained. "After the 1993 bombing of the World Trade Center, they installed a series of security cameras to record every vehicle that entered and left the parking garages of both towers. They also put cameras in the lobbies, near the elevators, and at all the entrances. If your boy was in the building, he was on one of those cameras." Jimmy paused and took a sip of his drink while watching Vince break into a smile.

"The problem," he continued, "is that all of the machines that recorded everything those cameras saw were inside the buildings." Jimmy didn't show it, but he took great delight in watching the smile fade from Vince's face.

"So how do we find out for sure that Tinsley was in the building?" asked Frankie.

"We wait, like everybody else," Jimmy replied. "They are planning to dig up every bit of those buildings, piece by piece. They are going to sort through all the evidence, all the body parts, down to the foundation. They're going to use DNA testing to identify every hand, toe, and ear they find."

"That could take months," said Vince, loud enough for the entire bar to hear.

Jimmy smiled. "It will probably take years," he said confidently.

"What do we do now?" asked Frankie.

Jimmy leaned forward. "The Feds have frozen all of his assets. If he's wandering around somewhere, he's going to need money. If he takes a job somewhere, we'll know. If he uses his credit card, writes a check, or uses his passport, we'll know. If he gets pulled over, if his car gets a parking ticket, we'll find out. We're keeping an eye on his home and on his wife. We've got their home phone and her office phone bugged. We're listening to conversations inside their home. The girl doesn't pee without us hearing."

"Let's squeeze the wife," said Vince suddenly. "If he's alive, she knows where he is."

Jimmy shook his head. "She either believes he's dead or she's one of the best actresses in town. Trust me, I have seen the faces of widows."

CHAPTER FIVE

The nightmare that had begun earlier in the week just kept getting worse. Jodi felt like she had fallen into a hole, but as she fell, the bottom kept getting further and further away from her. There didn't seem to be an end in sight as the light of day above her kept dimming. She wondered if she would ever feel normal again. She tried to remember what normal felt like.

For the first time in her life, she had no idea what to do or where to turn for help. She felt alone and abandoned, even when surrounded by friends and family. Her husband of nearly four and a half years was likely dead, but there was no way to confirm that. The attorney was telling her stories about a man she thought she knew, but the stories sounded like they were about somebody else, not the man she loved. She was probably going to lose her home and their investments. Charles carried a million-dollar life insurance policy, but that would be seized too. She had three hundred dollars in her credit union savings account and thirty-four dollars cash in her purse.

Just when she thought her situation couldn't get any worse, she was beginning to worry that she was pregnant.

She sat on an old suitcase in the basement and cried. She longed to hear his voice, to touch his face. She knew if he were here, he could explain to her the misunderstanding between himself and the Feds. He would be thrilled at the possibility that they might be having a child, and he would share in the anticipation and the excitement of finding out for sure.

Jodi would never forget the first time she saw him. He was young and dashing and full of confidence. She mistook his poised look for arrogance as he approached her and her friends in the crowded bar that night. She stood with a group of ladies that she thought were far more beautiful than herself, but his eyes were focused on her. When he spoke, he was kind and polite, asking her if he could buy her a drink and visit with her on the patio outside, in full sight of her friends, of course.

She started to say no, but her friend Jill interrupted and said that Jodi would love to have a drink with him. Then Jill added that she would be watching them carefully.

On the quieter patio, he introduced himself to her and told her that he had noticed her from the other side of the bar. He told her she was the prettiest woman in the room that night and that he couldn't help himself. He had to cross the bar to meet her. He was nothing like the other men who she had met. He didn't use a single pickup line, and he didn't talk about himself. He asked her question after question about herself and then follow-up questions after that.

When her drink was empty, he gave her a slight bow and asked if he could escort her back to her friends. "After all, you only agreed to one drink," he said.

She agreed to a second drink if he would tell her about himself. Before she finished her second drink, she was enamored with him.

***

He woke to the sun streaming through the window of his room. His back ached from the crummy bed at the Red Shutter Motel. He needed to move up to a slightly better class of motels, but he needed to make his cash last as long as he could.

Spreading his new map of Montana out on the bed, he picked a route to Kalispell. He would take Highway 12 to Avon, then 141 north to Highway 200. At Clearlake, he would turn onto Highway 83, skirt the eastern side of Flathead Lake, then follow the signs to Kalispell. It looked like a four-hour trip. By driving slowly, stopping at interesting places, and enjoying the scenery, he hoped to stretch the trip into an entire day.

Charles was unprepared for the beauty of the area as the road climbed out of Helena to the west. Every mile seemed to greet him with a more incredible view. The trees and the mountains seemed unending. He could smell the scent of pine trees in the air. He drove past ranch houses and barns that looked tired and weathered, but he thought every one of them was incredible. He stopped at every scenic turnout and wished he had brought his Nikon camera with him. Every direction was an award-winning photograph waiting to be taken.

Only a few days earlier, he looked at little homes that sat miles from nowhere and wondered why anybody would live like that. Now he envied the wide-open space that these people enjoyed. He wondered if these people had ever been to Brooklyn and what they would have thought of a million people living on top of one another.

As he drove through some of the most stunning country he had ever seen, he wished that Jodi was sitting close to him. He saw a woman sitting close to her man in the front seat of another pickup and became jealous. He had never owned a vehicle with a bench seat, and he laughed, thinking that BMW should look into that as an option. He stopped beside Nevada Lake and sat on the tailgate of the truck, enjoying the view while he munched on a bag of chips.

He couldn't get his mind off of Jodi. What would she say when she found out he was alive? He hoped she could someday forgive him for not letting her know he had survived. He hoped his reasoning for not contacting her was enough to make her understand. He ached to hear her voice, to let her know he was okay. He wanted so badly to stop at a payphone and to call her, but he knew that would only place her in danger.

***

Jodi hadn't been out of the house in six days. She felt the need to get out, to breathe, to go for a walk. She was ready to see the sunshine again. She wanted to go somewhere that she could see the broken skyline of Manhattan. She needed to see for herself that the towers were gone.

Unfortunately, the sunny weather of the last few days had yielded to rain clouds. Feeling the need to be alone, and knowing there would be a fight, she asked her mother to go to the store for a few things. When she left, Jodi wrote her a note saying she'd be back in a bit, then walked towards the Metro stop a few blocks from their home.

Leaving the brownstone with her head tucked under an umbrella, she passed a car parked just down the block. A man sat in the car reading the paper. Normally, she wouldn't have taken notice. She glanced over her shoulder after passing the car and could see the man looking at her in the rearview mirror. She walked a half block and looked back again. He wasn't following her. She told herself she was just being paranoid.

After riding the metro to the High Street, she walked about five blocks to the river. At the Brooklyn Bridge Park, tears filled her eyes while looking across the East River at the strange city. The towers had been there her entire life. They were supposed to always be there. She looked through the rain; they were really gone. She broke down in tears, knowing that he was really gone.

She sat on a wet park bench and let her umbrella fall to the ground. The soft rain fell against her face as she thought about Charles and his last moments. She hoped he had been at his desk, completely unaware of his fate. The reports said that his floor took a direct hit by American Flight 11. She prayed that he died instantly rather than living his last moments in pain or fear.

She didn't understand how he could have done the things he had done, cheating honest people out of their money so he and his mob clients could make huge gains. She didn't understand how the man she thought she knew had been so different. She put her face into her hands and sobbed as two men quietly walked past her.

A hundred feet beyond her, Jimmy White stopped and turned as if he was looking at the New York skyline as well. "That," he said to his associate who had been following her, "is a grieving widow. I don't think we need to tail her anymore. We'll keep an eye on her accounts, listen in on her conversations, and watch for the guy to pop up somewhere, but I'm ninety-nine percent sure he died over there."

***

Past Nevada Lake, Charles began to understand why there were so few roads in this part of the state. Road could only follow the rivers because the mountains were so high and the canyons so deep. The highway meandered along the river. It wasn't built for speed, it was built to get from one place to another eventually. He waved at a farmer on a tractor who was working a field next to the road, and the farmer waved back.

A half-mile ahead of him, he noticed a car on the side of the road. Its emergency flashers were blinking. He slowed and saw a woman and her young son struggling with the left rear tire. He didn't know why, but something compelled him to pull over to help. He hoped they wouldn't be frightened by him, and he hoped they weren't armed.

"Hi, do you need some help?" he asked.

The woman was about his age and very pretty. "Oh my gosh, yes. Thanks for stopping. We can't get the lug nuts loose."

Charles had never changed a flat tire in his life. In high school driver's education, they had watched the instructor do it, but that was fifteen or sixteen years ago. Luckily, the woman seemed to know what she was doing. When he put a little weight and a little more muscle than the petite woman could offer into the effort, all the lug nuts loosened. In a few minutes, they had the tire off and the spare on. The woman gave him a hug, and the boy shook his hand.

He got back into his truck, thinking, *That would have never happened in Brooklyn.*

There was something simple and honest and warm about the people out west. He wasn't naïve. He knew bad people existed everywhere, but the good people he was running into were different from those back in Brooklyn. They were more trusting and more open with strangers. He grew up assuming everybody was bad until they proved they were good. It seemed to be the opposite out west.

***

On her way home, she tried to remember the early symptoms of pregnancy. Nausea, fatigue, headache, backache, mood changes, and a missed period. She had them all, but she also knew they could all be caused by the stresses of her situation.

Stopping at the corner pharmacy, she spent ten dollars she didn't have on an early pregnancy test then walked home to dry off. The car down the street that held the man with the newspaper was gone. She didn't see anything else that seemed suspicious or different on her block.

Predictably, she caught hell from her mother for going out alone. She understood, the woman loved her more than life itself and was worried about her only daughter. "I'm fine, Mom. I didn't see a single hoodlum. Nobody tried to knock me off or rub me out or whatever the mob does in all those movies." Then she said matter-of-factly, "I'm going to go into work tomorrow for a bit."

"It's too early, Jodi," said her mother with a concerned look. "Give it some more time."

She hugged her and said, "I can't hide in here anymore. There are too many memories. I see him everywhere. I need to get out and do things that take my mind off him and everything else. I need to go back to work."

***

By the time he reached Lake Inez, the trees alongside the road had become tall and thick. Big, puffy thunderheads were forming above the mountains. They seemed to grow by the minute. He passed by Seely Lake, then stopped to look at the beauty of Swan Lake. He marveled at the color of the water and was jealous of the people who had cabins tucked around the lake. He watched with amazement as the clouds became more ominous.

Just past Swan Lake, the trees thinned, and the land opened to farming fields and meadows. The road turned west, taking him around the north end of Flathead Lake. He pulled off at the Flathead River boat ramp just in time to watch three boats scramble to get out of the water before the thunderstorms hit.

The winds came up first. Seemingly from nowhere, the reasonably calm day turned chaotic as the winds tore at the trees and whipped the river into a froth of whitecaps. A flash of lightning, closer than he had ever experienced, surprised him as he stood next to his truck. He thought the corresponding thunder clap was perhaps the loudest thing he had ever heard. Charles stood in absolute amazement as he watched limbs from trees being ripped and flung to the ground. Lightning hit the ground to the south of him. The bolts looked like brilliant daggers as they struck the earth. The thunder became a constant rumble, and he was unable to determine where one clap ended and where the other started.

Standing in awe and amazement, he forgot about his own safety. He knew one should never stand outside in a lightning storm, but he had never witnessed anything like the storm he was watching. He had watched hundreds of storms, but he had never been inside of one that packed such intense power.

He was shaken from his awestruck daze by a woman's scream. Glancing towards the boat ramp, he could see a couple trying to load a small fishing boat onto their trailer. The wind and the waves had blown the boat off the trailer, and as the man waded into the water to push it back straight another gust hit, knocking him down into the river. Charles ran to help. He manned the trailer's winch as the man stood and pushed the boat back straight. He didn't ask if they needed help; he simply jumped into action where he saw it was needed. He winched the bow up snug to the roller then stepped out of the way as the man hurried to the cab and pulled the boat out of the water.

He ran up the ramp to the tie-down area, where the man stopped and gave the woman a hand out of the boat as she stepped over the side. "Thank you," she said with a smile. He helped the man secure the tie-downs on the transom, finishing just as the rain hit.

The man reached into the cooler in the boat, took out two beers, handed him one, and ran for his truck, yelling, "Thanks, man!"

Charles ran to his own truck. He was soaked by the time he got inside. He watched the wind and the rain batter the area as he enjoyed an ice-cold Pabst.

***

Planning to only work a half day on the Monday after the Trade Center attacks turned out to be a smart move. Her first day back was consumed with emotional sympathy from her co-workers. People in the firm who she had very little interaction with in the past approached her desk and gave her hugs. A woman she didn't like brought her a bowl of candy, and the partners bought her a flower arrangement that was so large, it wouldn't fit in her cubicle.

They offered support, telling her that they were sure he would be found, but nobody had been pulled alive from the wreckage since the 12th. The news reported that all of the unidentified victims in the area hospitals had been named. She knew he was gone.

After five incredibly emotional hours in the office, she collected her things and quietly slipped out. The next day would be better, she hoped. Her well-meaning co-workers had done their duty; they had said the things to her that they felt they needed to say. Perhaps tomorrow she could just focus on work. She needed to focus on something, anything that would fill the tremendous emptiness she felt inside of her.

Jodi was exhausted by the time she got home. After speaking briefly with her mother, she went to her room to lie down for a bit. On the edge of the bathroom vanity, the unused pregnancy test seemed to taunt her. She picked it up and looked at it, then set it back down and went to her bed. She didn't cry; there were no more tears. She crawled onto the bed and sank back into a state of depression that had come to feel normal to her.

***

With the owner of the little house where he rented a room out of town, Damon Wilkes hosted a friendly poker game, inviting some of his friends. It was a small stakes game. Everybody bought in for twenty dollars. Damon wasn't much of a poker player and quickly blew through his chips. James came to his rescue. "I'll give you ten for those sick New York plates you got hangin' in your room."

Damon blew through those chips quickly too. He had a lot to learn about the game.

CHAPTER SIX

Wet and cold, Charles was happy to find the Best Western, Flathead Lake Hotel, just a few miles down the road. It was almost double the price he had been paying for a room, but he was ready for a better room and a better bed.

He took a long, hot shower and put on dry clothes. When he asked, the nice lady at the front desk gave him the name of two places to try for dinner, both less than a mile away towards the lake. She said the food was better at one than the other, but the people were probably nicer at the other. He couldn't remember which was which.

Charles was amazed when he stepped out into the parking lot. The skies had cleared, most of the clouds had moved to the east, the sun was shining, and it was cool but beautiful out. He hopped into the truck and drove towards Flathead Lake, quickly finding both the recommendations. Somers Bay Café was on his left, Del's was on his right. By visual observation, it looked like the food was probably better at the café. Del's looked like a tavern. He pulled into Del's.

After ordering a burger and a beer, Charles made a comment to the bartender that things were sure quiet, the place was nearly empty. "Well," said the lady, "it's not summer, and it's not Saturday night."

Charles remembered their trip to Key West to celebrate their first anniversary. They arrived on a Monday in the late afternoon. After checking in to a little bed and breakfast, Jodi said, "Let's go find a place to dance." He reminded her it was a Monday. They might not find a place to dance on a Monday night on the little island. Walking two blocks over to Duval Street, they were surprised to find bars packed full of people partying and having fun. He remembered fighting his way to the bar in the Hogs Breath Saloon and commenting to the bartender about the size of the crowd on a Monday night.

The bartender smiled and yelled back over the live music, "Welcome to Key West, where it's always Saturday night!"

In the much quieter Del's, he asked the bartender if she knew of anybody hiring for general labor type of work. She pointed to a table across the room. "That's John Gilmore over there in the plaid shirt. He's got a logging operation. You might ask him."

Walking across the room with his beer in hand, he stopped at the table. The three men quit speaking and looked up at him. "Mister Gilmore, I'm Will Roy. I'm looking for a job."

Gilmore looked him up and down before asking, "Have you ever worked in logging?"

"No, sir."

The man grimaced and scratched the back of his head while thinking it over. "I might have something in a week or two. Kind of a gofer position."

Charles smiled. "There's one more wrinkle. I've got some ex-wife problems back in Illinois. I need to work under the table, cash."

The husky logger smiled. "I've got some of those problems myself, but I only hire and employ people legitimately. I don't pay people under the table."

He thanked the man then asked him if he knew of anybody who might hire him, given his predicament. "Oh, I imagine that you can find something with some farmer or rancher up the valley. Good luck to you."

***

Jodi's second day at work was better. She only planned to work a half day but ended up spending most of the day at her desk. She had a lot of catching up to do. Her co-workers almost seemed to avoid her. The day before, they felt they had to offer sympathy; now it seemed they wanted to give her space. She enjoyed the lack of interruptions and got a lot of work done before her boss, one of the firm's partners, Eric Mills, asked her to come to his office.

Eric was a kind man. Out of true concern for her, he asked her how she was doing. She gave him her boiler plate answer that she was doing fine, it was hard, but she was going to get through it.

He saw through her charade. "How are you really doing?" he asked. "How about financially? Are you okay?"

She looked at him, determined to not let her guard down, then broke down in tears. She told him everything: the legal issues, the truth about her husband's practice, his lies to her, the worries about the DiPiero family, the frozen assets, and her financial issues.

Eric handed her a box of tissues then wrote down everything while asking a series of follow-up questions. Talking through it seemed to help take some of the burden off her chest, but it also put it all in perspective. She had a lot of problems in her life.

"The unfortunate part about Charles," he explained, "is the word 'probably.' If it was certain that he had died in the attack, we could appeal the freeze and likely separate his assets from yours. If they find his remains, the process can move forward. If they never find his remains, which is likely, given the ferocity of the fires and the collapse, he will need to be legally declared dead by absentia, which could take a long time."

He gave her a moment to compose herself before continuing. "With regard to the DiPiero family, I'm a water rights attorney. That's so far out of my realm that I don't have a clue on how to advise you."

He gave her a long look before saying, "The firm has a fund for purposes like this. I'll chat with the partners and see if we can get you some financial help."

"I'll be okay," said Jodi. "There are others who need help more than I do."

Eric smiled. It was just the response he expected from her. "Most of your household income has gone away, your life savings are frozen by the government. Your husband is missing in the largest terrorist attack in U.S. history. You've got a boatload of legal issues, and the Jersey mob might be pissed off at you. I can't think of anybody more deserving or more in need of help right now."

He stood and walked around his desk and gave her a hug. "We're going to help you get through this," he said as they embraced.

She buried her head into his chest. She longed to feel warm and secure. The cuddle was a little too long and a little too intimate to be just a consoling hug. She broke away after a few moments, said "thank you," and left his office feeling embarrassed.

***

Charles tossed and turned most of the night. His sense of guilt for leaving Jodi behind to deal with his legal troubles was nothing compared to the pain he knew she must be feeling. She wouldn't have any reason to believe he didn't die a horrendous death in a hell that he couldn't began to imagine.

He dreamt of her standing in the door of his office wearing a beautiful smile as the building exploded, the flames taking her from him. She screamed in pain as she disappeared in the inferno.

After waking, Charles made the ten-mile drive to Kalispell, the place he had targeted as his final destination based solely on the advice from a stranger in a Helena bar. Once there, he had no idea what to do. He drove the length of Main Street looking for a sign in the window of some business that said, "Help wanted, all employees paid in cash," but he didn't see it. He was impressed with the town. It was clean with tree-lined streets. American flags hung everywhere. He wondered if any of the flags flew daily from porches before the attacks.

Just beyond the middle of town, he spotted the Sykes Diner and stopped in for breakfast. Charles took a seat at the counter, one stool over from a middle-aged man who looked like a local farmer. He ordered a coffee and a big breakfast.

"Good coffee," he said to the man next to him.

"They do it up right here," said the man.

Charles took another sip. "Are you from the area?"

The man smiled. "Been here my entire life, except for a two-year vacation to Southeast Asia twenty years ago, compliments of the U.S. Army."

Charles turned and extended his hand. "Thank you for your service, sir."

The man shook his hand, saying, "It was an honor to serve my country, but I thank the lord each day that I made it home."

"This is a beautiful valley," replied Charles. "Do you happen to know of anybody looking for help, labor-type work?"

The man shook his head. "It's the end of the season, not much work around." He paused, and after a moment, said, "Ya know, there is a fella out towards my place who has a sign up on his gate post," he said. "The place is called the Big Sky Ranch. Used to be owned by Bob Beck, but about fifteen years ago, he sold it to an out-of-towner. I can't remember that guy's name. He used to run a bunch of cattle, but it been kinda quiet around there the last couple of years."

"Thanks. Where is this place?"

"Well, let's see. You're going to go a few blocks up this way to Idaho Street and turn east. Then you're gonna stay on that road for a few miles, out past the river and past Fred Price's place. The road turns south out at the little casino, but you're gonna keep going east, towards the mountains. That's called Lake Blaine Road. After a while, the road becomes Foothill Road. Now about a mile past where it turns south, look for Bench Drive. The Big Sky is up that road, big wooden sign over the entrance."

Charles looked at him for a moment with a blank stare, then said, "Go up to Idaho, turn east at the little casino, keep going east, and look for Bench Road after the road turns south."

"Yep," said the man.

After finishing his breakfast, he paid his bill and picked up the tab for the man next to him. "Thanks for the tip on the job. I'll drive out there and check it out."

He drove north on Main Street a couple of blocks then turned east on Idaho Street and followed it out of town. Three miles east of town, the road made a ninety-degree turn to the south at the Lucky Pick Casino. Charles laughed as he turned east onto Lake Blaine Road. The man had described the landmark as a "little casino." Tiny was a better description; the building looked like a doublewide trailer with wood siding under a pitched roof.

Driving east across the flat terrain, he was amazed at the mountain range ahead that abruptly rose from the valley, its peaks shooting towards the sky. He wasn't sure he would ever get used to the dramatic beauty of the area. He wondered if the locals still gasped in awe at the amazing scenery that surrounded them.

As he reached the tree line, the road turned south. After a mile or so, he saw the sign for Bench Road, so he turned left to follow it. It wasn't hard to find. Two large posts rose, holding a wood-carved sign that read "Big Sky Ranch." Nailed to the left side post was a store-bought red and black sign that said, "Help Wanted." There were no phone numbers or any other information. Charles chuckled to himself; it was exactly what he had been experiencing as he drove west. People out west seemed to give you the information you needed and nothing else. In New York, he thought to himself, the sign would have contained a job description, starting pay, and minimum job requirements. But this was Montana, and "Help Wanted" was enough said.

Charles needed the job and didn't want anybody else to show up while he was "interviewing." He stepped out of his truck and carefully removed the sign from the nail that attached it to the post before driving across the cattle guard and up towards the barn.

The road took him up a slight grade towards a huge red barn. Horses played in a corral on his right while a dozen head of cattle munched on grass in the pasture to his left. He could see a few outbuildings beyond the barn, and above it all, backed against the trees and framed by a majestic mountain, was a beautiful log cabin with a large porch that ran the length of the home. As the road turned to wind around the barn, he saw a man wearing a cowboy hat, jeans, and boots walking out of the barn towards him. Charles stopped, put on his cowboy hat, and stepped out of the truck carrying the help wanted sign.

Charles guessed the man was in his sixties. He wore jeans, a flannel shirt, a light jacket, and a tan cowboy hat that showed signs of sweat stains and years of use. He had a four- or five-day growth of stubble that didn't hide his aged face, which was creased and tarnished by his years in the sun and the wind.

"I see you're looking for help," said Charles, holding up the sign.

The man approached him, already assessing him by his clothes, his walk, and his old Ford pickup with the Illinois license plates. By the time he got close enough to shake the stranger's hand, he already knew something didn't add up. "I'm Mark Mulligan."

The two shook hands. "I'm Will Roy," said Charles. "I could sure use a job."

"Well, I could sure use some help. You ever worked on a ranch before?" asked Mark as they slowly walked back toward the pickup.

"Not ranches," said Charles. "I've pretty much worked on farms my whole life, out in Illinois. I'm a hard worker. You won't regret hiring me."

Mark walked over to the truck and leaned on the edge of the bed. "I sure need help, but I don't think you're going to work out for me."

"Can I ask why?" asked Charles with a questioning look on his face.

Mark rubbed the whiskers on his face before saying, "You can tell a lot about a man if you pay attention to the details. Your hands are soft, and I don't believe you've worked on a farm in years, if you ever have. You say you're from Illinois, but I hear New York in your voice; Queens, maybe Brooklyn. Your truck here isn't a farm truck. This thing hasn't been washed in years and yet there's not a piece of hay in the bed, not a weed, no bailing twine, and there's no mud up on the fenders. And that costume you got on, you're wearing the hat all wrong and you've obviously never walked on uneven ground in a pair of cowboy boots before."

Charles looked at the ground for a moment before looking the man in the eye. "Look, bottom line is, I need a job and I'll work my ass off to prove myself to you. I'll even work the first week for free. If you don't like me after that, I'll leave."

"Why don't you start with the truth?" said the crusty rancher. "Who are you and why are you here?"

Charles gave an apologetic look. "I need to live someplace where my reputation doesn't proceed me. I'm a first-world refugee. I made a lot of money in the dot.com market then lost most of it. I burnt out, I had all I could take, and now I'm nearly broke. If I didn't get away from it, I was going to be the guy on the evening news who jumped off the bridge. Now, with the World Trade Center thing, I don't know if the markets will ever recover, and frankly, I don't care anymore."

Mulligan stared at the man for several moments before saying, "Can you drive a tractor?"

"I can if you show me how," said Charles.

"Can you ride a horse?"

"I've been on a few pony rides in the park when I was a kid."

"Can you shoot?" he asked.

"I never have."

The rancher shook his head. "Have you ever done a day's work outside in the hot sun or the freezing cold?"

Charles looked at the ground. "No."

Mulligan gave a snort and shook his head. "Put your gear in the bunkhouse over there and hustle your ass back here to help me." Then he gave him a slightly irritated look and asked, "Do you even own a pair of work gloves?"

CHAPTER SEVEN

The police had been watching the area around South Chicago's Ogden Park following an increase in drug activities. Officer Brad Struck had been driving past the park at least once an hour during his night shift. He hoped the increase in police presence would send the dealers somewhere else.

Driving south on Racine Avenue past Bass Elementary School, he spotted a car in the school parking lot. Its interior lights shut off as soon as he saw it. He did a U-turn at Marquette Road and returned to check on the vehicle. As he approached the school, the car left the parking lot and drove north. He had no reason to be suspicious of the white Buick, thinking it was probably a teacher or an administrator working late at the school. Officer Struck had nearly dismissed the car until the driver turned left onto 64th Street at a high rate of speed.

Struck turned on his lights and siren and radioed in a pursuit in progress. The suspect car turned south on Peoria and east on 66th, then turned and shot south down an alley. He lost the car briefly, but two minutes later, found it crashed into a light pole at the White Castle. Two witnesses were pointing in the direction the man had run. Struck drove in that direction, but he wasn't able to find anybody who looked like they were trying to avoid him. He returned to the White Castle, where another officer was starting to process the scene of the accident and take information from the witnesses.

When he ran the New York license plates from the suspect car through the DMV database, he found they were assigned to a 1999 BMW sedan registered to the Clark

Financial Group in New York City. The BMW hadn't been reported as stolen, but when he ran the V.I.N number of the suspect's Buick, it came back as a stolen vehicle.

***

Charles worked side by side with Mulligan for the entire afternoon. First, they cleared old hay from the barn's loft, pushing it out the large door, then they swept it out. Once the loft was clean, they ripped up the old flooring, three-quarter-inch plywood, and replaced it. The rancher worked methodically; he didn't move quickly, but he also didn't stop. After spending the day moving a few tons of hay then removing the heavy old flooring and replacing it with even heavier material, Charles was spent.

He had tried over the last few years to work out a few days a week, but something always seemed to get in the way. His stockbroker muscles weren't used to real work. By the time they quit, as the light was getting too dim to see, he could hardly move.

"There's nothing in the bunkhouse to eat," said Mark. "Get cleaned up and settled then come up to the house and I'll fix something."

Charles dusted off his jeans and retrieved his cowboy hat from the nail he had hung it on then walked to the bunkhouse. The name of the building was accurate; it was a bunkhouse. There was nothing fancy or elaborate about the place. On one end of the large room was a bathroom, on the other end was a small kitchen and a table with six chairs around it. In the middle of the room stood a simple wood stove. Six bunk beds, a couch, and two old recliner easy chairs filled the rest of the room.

After cleaning up a bit, he walked up to the ranch house to join his new boss. His knock at the door was answered by an indiscernible yell from inside. He assumed it was Mulligan yelling for him to come in, so he opened the screen door and entered the home.

The living room of the home could have been right out of a country living magazine. Dark, hardy-looking leather furniture, a bear skin rug, and cowboy art adorned the room. A real wood fire was burning in the fireplace at the end of the room. Charles walked to his right, where he heard the sounds of a meal being prepared and found Mark in the kitchen.

"Take off your coat, open those cans of beans, then dice that onion." It was clear that Mark was the boss on this ranch; the time of day didn't matter. He hung his coat on the back of a chair before struggling with the can opener then making it clear to his boss that he had never diced an onion in his life.

"Is there no Mrs. Mulligan?" asked Charles as tears ran from his eyes while making a mess of the onion before him.

"There was once. She left me," said the rancher while stirring a hot frying pan filled with some type of meat. "I had a girlfriend for a quite a while, but she left last spring. Said if I wasn't going to commit, she wasn't going to stay around. What about you?"

Charles was unprepared to answer that question. "Well, I guess I'm technically still married. I haven't seen her in a while."

Mark said nothing in reply. He nodded while adding the beans to the skillet. "Tomorrow, I need to go into town. I'll have you move all that old flooring over to the old blacksmith shop, then load the old hay and I'll show you where to dump it."

"It's none of my business, but is there a reason behind the new floor in the hay loft?"

Mark smiled. "Sorry, my girlfriend used to tell me that when I get busy, I don't always share all the important details. I used to run a couple hundred head of angus here, now I'm down to just my breeding stock. The cattle business got pretty beat up over the years, but prices and demand seem to be on the rise. I'm doubling down, bringing in a small but expensive herd, and I'm getting back into the business. Hopefully, I'm ahead of the curve and ahead of the other ranchers in the valley."

After dinner, they shared a glass of whiskey by the fire in the living room. When Charles asked about his past, where he grew up, when he came to the valley, Mark abruptly changed the subject. When Mark asked Charles about his past, about his previous job and how the dot.com crash had wiped him out, he instead asked more questions about the ranch and the area. It was obvious to both men that neither wanted to talk about their past.

***

Jodi dreaded returning to the office after the awkward hug she had unintentionally shared with her boss. She tried telling herself that it was just her perception, that the hug had been normal. But burying her face into his chest while holding him tightly couldn't be mistaken as a normal hug. She thought about confronting him, apologizing for her actions, but then decided to act normal, business-like, as if nothing had happened.

They ran into each other at the coffee pot in the breakroom. He said "good morning" as if nothing out of the ordinary had happened. She felt relieved. Returning to her desk, she set upon the task of catching up from her time away but found herself still caught in the emotional fog of the last week. She found it hard to concentrate.

Images of Charles, buried under the rubble but still alive, haunted her. The rescuers at the World Trade Center site had not located a survivor since the 12th. They had converted from a rescue operation to a recovery operation. She knew there was almost no chance they would find him alive, but she couldn't give up hope yet.

Just before 11:00am, her phone rang. It was Eric asking her to come to his office. She told him she would be right there, then hung up the phone and buried her head in her hands. She tried to convince herself that he probably wanted to talk about something work related, but what would she do if he brought up the previous day's incident? Or worse, what if he mistook it for an advance and thought they might be starting some sort of extra-curricular relationship?

After working up her courage and thinking through her defense if he brought up the hug, she picked up her pen and pad and walked to his office.

"Have a seat, Jodi," he said in a business-like tone when she entered his office. She nervously sat across the desk from him. He finished writing something before turning his attention to her. "I spoke to the partners this morning about your situation. I didn't mention the legal matters concerning Charles, only your situation and your sudden lack of cash.

"The partners first wanted to pass along that they are keeping you and your family in their thoughts and prayers. They agreed that we would gladly offer the firm's services, pro bono, to help with any legal matters you might have stemming from the attacks and in the settlement of your husband's estate..." He caught himself and quickly said, "Should it come to that."

Eric slid an envelope across the desk towards her. "They also decided to give you a little bonus to help you with any financial issues you might have during this time. I had accounting convert it to cash so it doesn't get caught up in any of the red tape you're experiencing."

She felt overwhelmed. The envelope was thick. He had obviously gone to bat for her at the partners meeting while protecting her by not telling them the entire story. She resisted her urge to give him another hug. She thanked him and quickly left his office.

In a stall in the ladies' room, she composed herself then counted the cash, which totaled five thousand dollars.

***

Only a few miles from each other, looking at the same information over similar cups of coffee, FBI Special Agent Robert Anderst in his Midtown office and Jimmy White, across the river in New Jersey, tried to make sense of some confusing information. The license plates registered to Charles Tinsley's company car had just shown up on a National DMV search report. Both men were surprised that the plates weren't still attached to the silver BMW that each assumed was buried under a hundred million tons of debris in Lower Manhattan.

Jimmy White made a phone call to Illinois and found that the plates had been found on a stolen car in Chicago. Anderst didn't have time to follow up. He was busy chasing suspicious wire transfers from Dubai to a flight school in Florida. He set the DMV report aside, intending to include it with the DiPiero/Tinsley file when he had the opportunity.

While Anderst was accidentally but permanently misplacing the DMV report, Jimmy White was leaning back in his chair trying to think through all the possible circumstances that could lead to Tinsley's license plates showing up in Chicago. The obvious scenario was that Tinsley had survived, driven to Chicago, and either had his plates stolen or had acquired a different car and put his plates on it. White leaned forward and noted that on his legal pad. He jotted other possibilities on the pad. The car obviously hadn't been parked in the underground garage. Perhaps somebody had taken the opportunity to steal it and drive it four states away. Or someone may have stolen the plates off the BMW and they somehow ended up in Illinois.

Considering all the possible scenarios, the one that made the most sense was that Tinsley was alive and on the run.

***

It was another long day of back-breaking work. The sore muscles Charles suffered from the previous day seemed to get more painful with every sheet of plywood he lifted. When the flooring was moved and stacked, he started loading the old hay they had thrown down from the loft into a large hay wagon. Although he had never thought about the weight of hay, he was thinking about it now.

As he pitched the last fork of hay into the wagon, Mark drove up the lane and stopped near the barn. He got out of the truck and reached into the bed, then walked towards Charles with a twelve-pack of beer. "That's enough for today," he said as he tore open the end of the carton and handed him one. "I didn't figure you'd get it all done today. I'm impressed."

Charles reached for the beer, and with a thin smile, said, "I'm beat."

"It's a little different than day-trading, isn't it?" said Mark as he opened his beer.

"It's a lot harder on my back, but this office is certainly more beautiful than my office back home."

They sat on the edge of the hay wagon and looked down towards the valley while enjoying their beer. Mark told him about his plans to rebuild the corral, reroof the pole barn where he stored hay, and repair about ten miles of fence line. He smiled while handing his tired employee a fresh beer. "But you don't need to get those projects finished until tomorrow."

As the shadows grew longer, reaching east from the distant trees, a coyote trotted across the field below them. "That's probably the little bastard that got into my chickens a few months ago. That's why we don't have fresh eggs and fried chicken anymore. He only appears when I don't have the time or the interest in shooting him."

Hearing their voices, the coyote stopped and looked towards them. "How far can you shoot?" asked Charles.

"Well, with the 30-30 saddle gun I carry in the truck, and my old eyesight, that's a long shot. What do you figure, about two hundred, two hundred fifty yards? But I have a couple of rifles up at the house with scopes. That would be a pretty easy kill."

Charles took a sip of this beer. "I've never held a real gun."

Mark turned and gave him a surprised look before reaching under his coat and retrieving a pistol from his shoulder holster. He pulled back the action, kicking a shell out of the chamber, then handed it to Charles. "It's completely safe; there's no way it can fire now. But always treat every gun as though it's loaded."

Holding it, Charles was surprised at the weight. He held it carefully, away from his body, like a hand grenade that might go off at any time.

"Don't be scared of it," said Mark. "Hold it in your right hand with your pointer finger outside the trigger guard. The only time your finger goes inside that trigger guard is when you have a target in your sights." He showed him how to use his left hand to steady the weapon, then how to line up the sights with a target. "Want to give it a try?"

"Sure," said Charles tentatively.

Mark slid off the wagon and walked towards the corner of the barn. "Now before you get too fancy and try to hit anything, I want you to fire a round at the hillside over there." He showed him how to jack a round into the chamber, then made him hold the gun as he had shown him, both hands, elbows bent, leaning slightly forward. "When you're ready, squeeze the trigger gently."

The sound of the big Glock .45 surprised him more than the kick. "Wow, that's a lot louder than I would have suspected," Charles said over the ringing in his ears.

Mark laughed. "Remove your finger from the trigger guard and keep that thing pointed down range. It's cocked and ready to fire again." He instructed him on how to lower the hammer without firing the gun. "Now are you ready to try and hit something?"

He set up two empty beer cans on a wood rail fence and moved Charles to a spot about fifteen yards from them. "There you go. Knock 'em off there."

Charles looked at him. "That's a little close, isn't it?"

"Well, this is a hand gun. It's not designed for long range. I'll teach you how to shoot a rifle one of these days. I'll bet you this week's pay that with your next four shots, you can't hit either one of those cans. You miss, and you get nothing, like we agreed. You hit one, and at the end of the week, I'll pay you."

Charles raised the weapon. Mark calmly told him to move his right elbow closer to his body and reminded him to line up the sights on the target and to squeeze the trigger. Then he told him to pull back the hammer, take a deep breath, and fire when he was ready. He missed with his first shot, hit a can with his second, and knocked the other can off with his third shot.

"Wow, the boy's a natural," said Mark as he took the weapon away from him. "Normally, I'd call that beginner's luck, but you sure hold that gun steady. How's your eyesight?"

"It's always been 20/20," said Charles.

"It shows," replied Mark. "I picked up some food for the bunkhouse, but fixing dinner last night reminded me that I miss cooking. I'm going to make Osso Bucco tonight. Get cleaned up and come up to the house in about an hour."

***

Jodi had immersed herself in her work. Her subconscious mind had realized that being buried in riparian owner's rights, irrigation easements, and their conflict with the eminent domain clause of the Fifth Amendment was calming. Her brain took a break from the events of September 11th, her husband, and all the issues created by his business practices.

She was so engrossed in her work that she didn't actually hear her co-workers tell her goodnight or realize they had all left hours earlier. Eric Mills cleared his throat after standing next to her desk, unnoticed for nearly fifteen seconds.

"Oh, Eric. Geez, what time is it?" she asked while noticing that most of the office lights were off and it was very quiet.

"It's almost eight. You need to knock off and get out of here," he said in a concerned voice.

"Wow, I got so buried in getting caught up that I didn't realize everybody had left."

"Yeah, it's just you and me and the cleaning people here now. I'm going to walk over to Sofia's and grab a quick salad for dinner. Would you like to join me?"

For some reason, while her brain was saying "no," her mouth said "yes." He left her cubicle to retrieve his coat and briefcase while she sat in her chair trying to come up with an excuse to get out of dinner. Unable to think up a good one before he returned, she walked with him to the elevator then a block down the street to a little Greek restaurant.

The tiny restaurant only held ten tables crowded into a little space off the boulevard. They did a big take-out business for both lunch and dinner. It had become a favorite of the law firm's employees. The owner recognized them both immediately and walked them to an open table. Without asking, he brought out hot bread and poured them two glasses of Agiorgitiko, a Greek red wine.

They sipped their wine and tore off pieces of bread while engaging in mundane conversations about cases they were working on. The awkwardness was evident to both of them. When they reached for the bread at the same time and touched hands, Eric pulled his back too quickly. He smiled and decided to address the discomfort they were feeling.

"I'm sorry about the hug I gave you yesterday. I didn't mean for it to last so long, but we've worked together a long time, and I really do care about you as a person. I guess I wanted to hug away all your problems and worries."

Jodi blushed. "Thank you for saying that. I guess I needed something that's suddenly missing in my life, the embrace of a man. I didn't want you to think I was being inappropriate either."

He looked at her. She was beautiful, sexy, and vulnerable. He chose his words carefully. "I have complete and total respect for you. I would never intentionally be inappropriate in any way. But if you ever feel the need for a hug, just a hug, I'd be happy to help out. You have a lot going on in your life. I want to be there for you."

She smiled and looked at the table, uncertain what to say other than "thank you."

Sipping on a glass of ouzo at the three-stool bar just twenty feet away from them, Jimmy White wished he could hear what they were saying. The attorney's expression was sincere and kind, but White thought he saw the man take a quick glance towards her cleavage when she looked away. He could tell she was blushing and seemed less than comfortable with the conversation, but she also didn't seem in a hurry to leave. It was certainly a fascinating twist to an interesting situation.

CHAPTER EIGHT

Every muscle hurt when Charles got out of bed in the morning. He had spent another night freezing his ass off because he couldn't get a fire to light in the woodstove. He wasn't about to admit to Mark that he didn't know how to make a simple fire, but he was almost out of wooden matches. He had nearly gone through a full box along with every piece of paper and cardboard he could find in the bunkhouse. His results had been the same: the room would fill with smoke from the burning paper while failing to ignite the pieces of wood in the stove.

Charles had his coat on, with the collar pulled up around his neck while making a pot of coffee, when Mark walked in. The cowboy immediately recognized the issue. It was colder inside than outside, and it was obvious the room had been filled with smoke. He didn't want to embarrass his new employee by bringing attention to his lack of fire-building abilities. Besides hunting and gathering, it was one of the most manly of the primal skills every male should possess. He took a different tack.

They talked about the chores for the day while waiting for the coffee to brew, then with a fresh cup of coffee in his hands, Mark said, "Hey, it's gonna get cold tonight. That stove can be a bitch to get lit. Let me show you how." He kneeled in front of the stove and cussed, complaining that the last guy who stayed there hadn't cleaned out the stove. Mark remembered cleaning it himself just a month earlier.

He showed Charles how to open the damper on the stove pipe, then instructed him on how to cut kindling with the hatchet. He found an old newspaper in the bottom of the wood box and showed him how to wad it, put the kindling on top, light it, then wait for the kindling to start popping before gradually adding larger pieces to the fire. Once the fire was burning, he instructed him on how to bank the fire, adjusting the damper and the stove door's air flow regulator so the fire would burn slowly through the night.

Charles watched with great interest then commented, "Yeah, that's different from the stoves I'm used to." Mark turned away and smiled.

They spent the day finishing the barn project, which included wiring some new lighting and repairing the track on the large sliding doors. Charles was happy to have a respite from the back-breaking work of the last two days.

As Charles was sweeping up after their final project for the day, Mark said, "I'll set up some targets on the hillside over there and you can try shooting my old 30-30."

Mark was again an excellent instructor. He threw his jacket over the corral fence and showed him how to use it as a rest. He described the old lever-action saddle rifle's different parts to him and then told him again how to line up the sights, breathe, then squeeze the trigger. Charles picked up the skill of shooting a rifle quickly. His perfect eyesight and steady hand made it easy to hit the targets. "Tomorrow, we'll move them out further and see how good you really are," said Mark.

Charles admired the rifle. "This is a beautiful gun. You said this was old. How old is it?"

"1904," said Mark as casually as if it was built yesterday.

***

Dinner with the DiPiero brothers was always interesting. Jimmy White knew the evening would be unusually entertaining based on what he had to tell them. He arrived on time and took a booth in the back corner of the restaurant. As usual, they showed up about fifteen minutes late, accompanied by their driver/bodyguard, a younger man who Jimmy knew was their nephew.

Jimmy's assessment of their hired muscle was low. He was overweight, slow, and thought he was tougher than he was. He looked like the big bully in school who nobody challenged because of his size. Because he had never been challenged, he really didn't have much in the way of real fighting ability or aptitude. Jimmy knew in a pinch the kid would be worthless.

The bodyguard sat at a table nearby, Vince and Frankie joined Jimmy at his table.

"What do you have?" asked Vince impatiently while the waiter was pouring the brothers wine from the two bottles Jimmy had ordered.

"A new development," Jimmy replied while tipping his head towards the waiter, indicating to the brothers that he wanted to wait until they could talk in private.

When the waiter walked away, Jimmy continued. "The license plates off Tinsley's BMW were recovered on a stolen Buick in Chicago."

Vince slammed his hand down on the table, jostling the wine glasses. "I fuckin' knew he was alive. I could feel it. Let's go get him."

Jimmy raised both his hands. "We don't have any other evidence to support that he is alive yet. All we know is his car wasn't in the parking garage under the North Tower when it collapsed. I have thought through all the possible scenarios. I think the most likely one is that he is alive and on the run. My associates in Chicago haven't had any luck locating him."

"I'll go find him myself and then he'll wish he had died a nice calm death in the towers," said Vince as his veins popped out of his forehead and neck.

Jimmy smiled. "If he's hiding in Chicago, you'll never find him by looking. He's screwed up once. If he's still alive, he'll screw up again, and then we'll deal with him."

Frankie turned to his younger brother. "Let the man do his job. We've got our own problems here. I don't need you running off to Chicago to hunt for some ghost. Jimmy will find him for us."

"What about the wife?" asked Vince. "Let's nab her and make her talk."

"If Tinsley's alive," said Jimmy. "I don't think she knows about it. I sat twenty feet from her last night, and she still acts like a grieving widow."

Frankie waited for his brother to calm down before he dropped his bombshell. "There's something else," he said to the two of them. "I just found out that before the markets closed on September tenth, Tinsley sold all of our shares of a Nevada Real Estate Investment Trust. The proceeds from that sale aren't in any of our accounts."

"Are you saying that bastard stole money from us?" said Vince as the veins reappeared.

Frankie tried to remain calm. "I'm not sure he stole the money. It might be sitting somewhere waiting for somebody to push it into our accounts. But there is nobody to call; his entire company is gone."

Jimmy White removed a pen and a small notebook from the inside pocket of his suit jacket. "I'll look into it. How much money is missing?"

"Two point seven million," said Frankie. Vince looked like he might be having a heart attack.

***

Nights were the worst. At night, it was quiet, and Jodi was alone with her thoughts. At night, she could see his face, twisted with anger as he walked away from her that last time. She could imagine his final, horrible moments. She wondered if he was thinking of her as he died.

Never in her life had she felt such loneliness, such an emptiness inside of her. She was almost certain she was pregnant, but she was unable to make herself use the drugstore pregnancy test. Positive or negative, the results would be both good and bad news. She would either be a poor, single mother of a beautiful little fatherless child or she wouldn't be pregnant. She wouldn't have to raise a baby in this crazy world, but she would probably spend the remainder of her life alone and lonely.

The hole in her heart was big enough to drive a bus through. Her thoughts were so scattered, she couldn't sleep. She lay in their bed, wishing he was there. Her waking nightmare would continue until exhaustion overtook her, then the nightmares in her sleep would wake her in a cold sweat. She hated the nights.

Twenty-four hundred miles away, Charles battled with demons of his own. In the darkness of the bunkhouse, the only sound was the crackling of the fire in the woodstove as he thought of her. He wondered what she was feeling, what hell was she experiencing when she imagined the horrific death she thought he had experienced. How would he explain to her why he had left her, without even a phone call, without a hint of hope that they would be together again someday?

He wanted so badly to hear her voice. He wanted to explain to her that he had screwed up. His entire career had been screwed up. He should have walked away the day Uncle Ed told him what they did, but he let his greed overrule his morals. He had tried to build a legitimate business. He opened accounts for friends and families, but in the end, greed won. He had to keep the engine running on the business that had made him wealthy. He couldn't give his wife the beautiful home she deserved by managing fifty-thousand-dollar accounts for school teachers and taxi drivers.

A light rain started falling. The sound of it pattering on the bunkhouse's tin roof was soothing. As he fell asleep, he wondered if she could ever forgive him. He had been such an asshole.

***

Mornings had quickly become his favorite time of the day. In the cool mountain air of the Rockies, he woke early and seemed to be refreshed and ready to take on the day. Mornings brought new opportunities and possibilities.

Charles was up with the sun. He brewed a pot of coffee and made scrambled eggs, bacon, and toast. He was just finishing making breakfast, when he heard Mark's boots on the wooden porch outside. "You're just in time," he said as Mark walked in.

"Wow, smells good," said the older cowboy.

Over coffee and breakfast, they made a plan for the day. They needed to bring some irrigation line up from the lower eighty and then fix a gate on the little corral. After that, Mark would show him how to repair barbwire fence. Charles would start the task of mending fence line around the fifteen hundred acres that was the Big Sky Ranch.

"You won't be able to get to it all by truck," warned Mark. "Some of it is only accessible by horseback or foot because of the terrain and the brush." He smiled. "I'm going to have to teach you to ride."

Charles laughed. "By the time you're done teaching me to shoot, and ride, and mend fence, I'll be a real cowboy."

Mark smiled. "Every man, deep down, at some level, wants to be a real cowboy. Hollywood glorified the profession like none other. Men want to ride the open range with a six-gun on their hip. They want to be free to work in the sun, drink whiskey in saloons, and swagger down Main Street like John Wayne. Women want to try to wrangle themselves a cowboy. They love the rugged, free-spirited nature of the man. The problem is, once they capture him, they want their cowboy to stay home and be near them. Women fall for the man, then try to change him. The cowboy feels fenced in, miserable, then the woman falls out of love with the man pulling weeds in her garden. It's a century-old problem."

"Wow," said Charles. "You've put a lot of thought into that."

Mark shook his head. "I've had a lot of experience in it." He finished the eggs and toast on his plate before saying, "Hey, speaking of women. I'm meeting a gal, probably the last lady in the valley who doesn't hate me. We're going to go dancing on Saturday night. You should come along. It would do you good to spread your wings a bit and get off the ranch."

"I wouldn't want to get in your way," said Charles.

"It's not a date. We just agreed to meet at this joint up near Columbia Falls to do a little dancing. If we hit it off, there might be a little romancing, but she's already brought up my 'love 'em and leave 'em' reputation. It might not go anywhere."

"Well, that sounds good," said Charles. "I'll come watch a master working at his craft. Maybe I can pick up a few tips on how to woo the fairer sex."

"I'll show you how to fail, then you can do the exact opposite," said Mark as he stood and finished his coffee with a last swig. "Let's get to it. Take my truck and go hook up the pipe trailer that is parked next to the shop. Then pick me up down by the barn and we'll go get that pipe loaded."

Charles put the dishes in the sink, turned off the coffee maker, then grabbed his jacket, hat, and gloves before heading out the door. He walked over to Mark's big Dodge truck and hopped into the driver's seat. The keys were in the ignition, but he recognized a problem before he even touched them. He got back out of the truck and walked down to the barn.

"Problem?" asked Mark when he saw him approaching on foot.

"Yeah. I don't know how to drive a stick."

"You're shitting me," said Mark with a grimace. He let out a heavy sigh, then pointed towards the distant truck, saying, "Let's go learn how to drive a manual transmission."

***

Paper and electronic trails of transactions in the U.S. financial markets were highly regulated. It was almost impossible to hide money. Jimmy White had unraveled complicated transactions before; normally, it was an easy process. When a security sells, the proceeds go to a clearing house at the Federal Reserve Bank. From there, the funds are routed to the correct brokerage firm account and then to the investor's account.

At 8:45am on the morning of September 11th, the computer servers at Clark Financial Group along with all the supporting documentation regarding the transaction were destroyed. The clerks who processed the transaction and filled out the log books had likely died. The DiPiero's shadow trusts named "Continental XP-4579 Irrevocable Trust" didn't own the shares any longer. The proceeds from the sale had been disbursed, but the money had seemingly vanished.

Digging too deeply into the disappearance of the funds might trigger an SEC investigation into the trust. Such an examination could reveal the true owners of the trust and put the rest of their funds at risk. It was a can of worms that probably wasn't worth opening. Finding a few million dollars could cost them a hundred million. White would suggest that they forget about the funds from the sale of the Real Estate Investment Trust. Frankie would agree, Vince would blow a cork.

***

After killing the truck's engine for the third time, Charles started the motor again. He let the clutch out slower while pressing a little more on the accelerator and got the truck moving in first gear. Mark made him stop and start ten times before they ventured out onto the open road, where he allowed him to try second gear. Returning to the ranch, he had trouble backing up to the trailer, then nearly hit the corner of the shop building with the trailer as they pulled away. Mark tried his best to be patient, but his patience was running thin.

As they drove down to the land known as the "lower eighty," Charles asked an obvious question. "So why did you hire me?"

"I needed the help," said Mark.

"Yeah, but there's got to be guys around who can fix fence, light fires, ride horses, and drive stick shifts."

Mark took off his hat, ran his hand through his thinning hair, then put the hat back on. "Well, to tell you the truth, I don't have a very good reputation in the valley. When I first bought the ranch, I was an out-of-towner. That alone pissed off some people. The foreman and I had a disagreement on how things worked around here, so I fired him. Turns out he was kind of a popular guy around town. Then it got worse. The previous owner had always bought his alfalfa from Bud Smutz down the road here. I searched around a little and got a much better deal from a farmer over in Marion. I didn't anticipate the shit storm that would create.

"Just when I thought things were getting better, I met Kristine, a hairdresser in town. We dated for a while, then she moved in. When things went bad, she moved out and told every woman in town what an asshole I was."

"Wow." Charles laughed. "You couldn't win."

"The final straw," said Mark with a shake of his head, "was in the mid-nineties when the big corporations were getting into farming and ranching. When John Cougar and his friends started doing Farm-Aid concerts, I decided to sell off most of the stock. I let my hands go and hunkered down until ranching got better. Everybody decided that I didn't know what the hell I was doing. They all kept doing what they had always done, but they lost money doing it. A bunch of the local ranchers went bankrupt."

"But you're still here," said Charles.

Mark smiled. "Yep, I'm still here. Half the ranchers in the valley don't like me, the other half don't care one way or another. But I'm still here and I've got a guy working for me who seems to want to work hard and learn the job. Together, I think we can rebuild a pretty solid cattle operation on the Big Sky."

Charles put his hand up for a high-five. Mark returned a hearty slap.

***

Vince DiPiero had never been one to forgive or forget a grudge. When he was in his mid-thirties, he ran into a guy who had been mean to him in the seventh grade. Vince beat the hell out of the man in a Newark disco then left with the guy's date.

The junior high upper-classman had only called him names and spit on him. Charles Tinsley had stolen $2.7 million dollars, sat for a sworn deposition with the FBI, and turned over records of his family transactions to the SEC. Vince thought a quick death was too good for Tinsley.

Vince believed Jimmy White was a waste of time and money. In the past, White had been hired to eliminate a rival or a deadbeat, but they had always been easy targets to find and easier to kill. His fancy talk and expensive suits didn't impress Vince. In Jersey, vengeance was served in dark alleys by tough guys in leather jackets with fists and knives.

Frankie was right, as much as Vince hated to admit it. They had a lot going on and he needed to be in town, not chasing shadows in Chicago. Then he thought of Huey. Maybe it was time to let the kid prove himself.

Hubert Tinsley was Vince's nephew, his big sister's kid. Growing up, he had always been large for his age. Vince liked the kid; he was a mean son of a bitch. When he dropped out of high school, Vince had put him to work and started grooming him. Huey started working for them when he was seventeen, doing general labor on the docks. In his early twenties, Vince had him do some collection work, picking up rents and loan payments from various people around town. Now he collected payments, drove the brothers around town, and wasted a lot of time standing around looking menacing. Although Frankie wouldn't admit it, similar to Vince, he liked the image the kid portrayed. He enjoyed having a tough guy standing in the background. The brothers seemed to receive a higher level of respect, or fear, when Big Huey was standing in the corner with a mean look and a bulge under his jacket.

The truth was different from reality. Jimmy White's assessment of the kid had been spot-on. Huey grew up blessed or cursed with a huge frame. In first grade, he was at least four inches taller than any other kid in his class, and through his school years, he was always the biggest kid around. He quickly learned that his size intimidated his school mates and even some of his teachers. He learned to use that to his advantage as he shook down kids for their milk money and enjoyed food from their lunches.

As a freshman in high school, some of the seniors started calling him Baby Huey, a name he hated. They taunted him, wanting to test him to see if he was really as tough as he acted. Huey felt backed into a corner; he thought he might have to fight for the first time in his life, when a fortunate event occurred. One night, a senior football player involved in the teasing got jumped by a rival team as he walked home alone. His beating and resulting concussion was so severe that he had no memory of it. Somebody incorrectly credited Huey with the beating and his reputation as a tough guy was cast.

Armed with a pocket full of cash and an earful of advice from his uncle on how to find Tinsley, Huey boarded a flight out of Newark to Chicago. He stayed in a nice hotel, took in a few sights, and hung out in some seedy clubs. He kept his eyes peeled for Tinsley the entire time he was there; he even asked around. Nobody, not the strippers in the clubs, the bouncer at the bar, or even the pretty lady at the front desk of his hotel knew who Tinsley was. He returned to New Jersey empty-handed except for stories of his time spent in the dark underbelly of Chicago.

CHAPTER NINE

At a little restaurant two blocks from her office, Jodi met with Mac Telford to discuss her husband's legal issues. "Given the unusual circumstances surrounding Charles and the Trade Center attacks, I was able to get the SEC to release your personal checking and savings accounts," said the attorney. "That should give you enough money to make ends meet."

Jodi felt like a huge weight had been lifted from her shoulders. "Thank you so much. That will help out more than you know."

Mac took a sip of his wine before continuing. "The large investment accounts will remain frozen. If the court rules unfavorably, you will likely lose those accounts, forfeit any life insurance, and lose your home."

She looked down at her plate and shook her head, then asked, "Why would he do what he did?"

"Work with the mob? Intentionally inflate stock values then dump his clients' shares for huge gains?" asked Mac. "Charles and I talked about his business relationship with the DiPiero family a few weeks ago. When he told me about his uncle's business, he said he simply continued doing what his uncle had always done. He knew what he was doing was wrong, even illegal. But it was what he knew, and it was certainly profitable. Honestly, I think he did some of it for you. He mentioned that he thought you deserved a nice home and nice things."

Mac saw the questioning look in Jodi's eyes when she looked up. He continued, "As far as the penny stock schemes, I think Charles was an incredibly smart and extremely competitive man. I don't think he saw the damage he did to other investors while he was making incredible gains on his own funds. In business, some win, some lose. Charles was a winner."

He handed her the handkerchief from his suit coat pocket when he saw a tear welling up in her eye. "He was a good man who made some bad decisions," said Mac. "I think you need to remember the good husband, not the businessman."

She gave him a little smile. "He was an amazing husband. He was a loving man who worked hard and made me laugh every day."

"Don't ever forget that man," said Mac as he reached across the table and patted her on the hand.

***

They knocked off work mid-afternoon on Saturday, which was just fine with Charles. Between the two of them, they had decided that they might need to use the old blacksmith shop in the near future to house welding equipment and do light repairs. Charles spent most of the day moving the old barn flooring he had stacked there to a trailer, then up to a shed near the big pole barn.

After showering, he walked over to the main house and enjoyed a beer in the sun on the big porch. When Mark was ready, they drove into town and enjoyed a good dinner before driving north to the Blue Moon Dance Hall outside of the little town of Columbia Falls.

The Blue Moon, Mark explained, was an old Flathead Valley staple. It had been around since the forties, but during the tourist season, it was best avoided. When the tourists left at the end of the season, the locals would hang out there again. From the outside, Charles wasn't sure he wanted to go in. The weathered building looked sketchy. After entering, a woman waved to them as they moved to the middle of the barroom. Mark pointed and waved to Charles to follow him.

Brenda, Mark had explained, was a widow of an oil executive who had died of cancer several years back. They had been introduced by a mutual friend and had agreed to go out dancing once she returned from a month-long trip to her home on Kauai.

The tall, slender woman stood to give Mark a hug and then over the music introduced them to her friend Suzanne before Mark introduced Charles, or Will as he knew him, to the two women. They ordered a round of beer and tried to visit, but the band was too loud to accommodate much conversation. After a bit, Mark turned, smiled at Charles, then he and Brenda got up and headed towards the dance floor, leaving Charles and Suzanne in an awkward situation.

Leaning over towards the woman who was probably twice his age, he said, "I'd ask you to dance, but I honestly don't know how to dance like this."

"Oh hell, honey," said the woman. "I can teach you to dance. Come on!"

Without a chance to argue, she was up and dragging him out onto the dance floor. As Suzanne led, teaching him what to do, Charles noticed that Mark and Brenda seemed to make good partners. They looked like they had been dancing together for years. Charles stepped on Suzanne's feet, he turned the wrong direction, picked up with the wrong hand, and generally screwed up. But Suzanne was a good instructor, and after five songs, he was starting to get down both the two-step and a few swing moves.

They returned to their table when the band took a break. The ladies went to the restroom while the men ordered another round. As they sat at the table, a beautiful, tall, late-twentyish brunette in a cowboy hat, button-up white shirt, and Wranglers that looked like they had been painted on, walked by and gave Charles a smoky look.

"Good God, man," said Mark as he slapped Charles on the shoulder. "If that wasn't an invitation to dance, I don't know what is."

Charles smiled. Several years ago, before he was married, he would have been up and chasing the beautiful woman across the bar. All that her flirtatious look had done was reminded him of how much he missed his wife. In an attempt to take his mind off Jodi and the pain he must have inflicted on her, he drank too much and danced the night away with Suzanne, a woman old enough to be his mother.

***

It was just going to be drinks on Saturday night with Jodi's friends and some co-workers. She didn't know that Eric had been invited until she got to the pub. By the end of the night, as people shuffled around the table as they do, her boss ended up on the stool next to her. Jodi should have moved away when his knee touched hers under the table. A part of her felt that moving away would make the situation even more awkward than it already was, part of her craved human touch. And it was just knees touching under a table in a crowded bar. She even thought that he might not have a choice, that Cassandra, who sat on the other side of him, might be crowding him.

For the first time in a couple of weeks, she laughed with her friends. It was an evening out she needed. Nobody noticed that she was drinking soda water with lime except for the waitress.

Eric Mills wasn't a bad person. He had been attracted to the young paralegal from the day she started at the firm but kept everything professional because she was married, and he respected that. But when her husband became a victim in the Trade Center attacks, he was quick to jump to her side. His intentions were honorable, for the most part. He would be there for her in her grief. He would help her in any way he could, and maybe one day, down the road, his efforts would pay off.

It was a little after eleven when the group began to split up. Rain had started to fall, and Jodi hadn't brought an umbrella. "I'm parked just around the corner," said Eric. "Let me get my car and I'll give you a ride."

"It's only four blocks," said Jodi.

"It's really starting to come down. Wait here and I'll pull up in front," he replied without giving her a chance to argue.

As they pulled up in front of her home, he asked, "Is there anything you need? Do you have a lightbulb out you can't reach, a dripping faucet that's driving you nuts? Anything?"

"No," she said with a smile. "You've done so much already, more than you know." She reached over and gave him a long hug, then a little peck on the cheek before she climbed out of the car and ran for the door.

He watched her run up the steps. She turned and gave a little wave after unlocking and opening the door. He smiled to himself while thinking that he might not have to be as patient as he originally thought.

***

Sitting alone in front of his fireplace, enjoying a snifter of brandy and the first fire of the season, Jimmy White tried to figure out what Vince DiPiero had been thinking. An associate in Chicago had called him earlier in the evening telling him that some big, dumb kid had been snooping around the clubs in Chicago trying to find Tinsley. It was a task White had assigned to his associate, somebody he trusted to find the man if he was there, without alerting Tinsley that people were searching for him.

Tinsley would eventually surface if he was still alive. But the brothers were impatient, which made White nervous. A large part of his job was to protect the family from the law, their rivals, and themselves. If the brothers continued to do stupid things, he wouldn't be able to protect them. White knew that he had to find the stock broker quickly.

The question was, where did he go? White hadn't found any reason for him to go to Chicago. He didn't seem to have friends or family there. The best he could tell, the guy had never been to Chicago before. He might have exchanged the New York plates for Illinois tags and kept moving. He might have dumped the car and kept going. But where?

Maybe Vince was right. Maybe he should grab the wife. She might not know anything, but if Tinsley had contact with anybody in New York, he would quickly find out they had her and probably tip his hand. White grimaced. It was a one-way street. Once they grabbed her, there was no turning back. She would have to die as well.

Patience was the key, but the lock was really starting to rattle.

***

Charles had never been a heavy drinker. He enjoyed a cocktail or two after work on occasion, maybe some wine with dinner, but he could count on one hand the times that he had been really drunk since college. He lay in his bunk with an incredible hangover, well after sunup, until he heard those familiar boots coming up the steps and across the porch of the bunkhouse.

Mark didn't say a word. He started a pot of coffee and then put some bacon in a frying pan. While the bacon was frying, he peeled a couple of potatoes then used a grater to shred the potatoes into another frying pan. He poured some of the grease from the bacon on top of the potatoes then seasoned them with garlic salt and pepper. After pouring two cups of coffee, he reached into his back pocket and removed a flask, then poured a decent shot into each. He set one cup on the little table next to Charles' bunk and sat in a rocking chair near the woodstove, opening it to see if there were any coals.

"Too late in the day to build a fire," he said.

"I think I drank too much," said Charles with a groan.

Mark chuckled. "I'm pretty certain that Suzanne was trying to get you drunk. I think she was hoping for a little action with Cowboy Will."

Charles sat up in his bed and reached for the coffee cup before saying, "Ah geez, she kissed me on the mouth."

"Well, that's after you grabbed her ass on the dance floor," said Mark with a big laugh.

"I'm never drinking again," promised Charles with a frown.

After two cups of coffee spiked with whiskey, some eggs, bacon, and hash browns, Charles thought he might survive. "You do the dishes, then get your boots on. I'll be back in fifteen or twenty minutes," said Mark.

Charles just wanted to crawl back on his bunk, but he knew that his hangover was self-induced, and he would be expected to buck up and put in a day's work. He had just finished the last of the dishes and left them in the strainer to dry, when he heard a noise out front. He pulled on his boots and found his jacket on the floor under the hook near the door. His hat was across the room where he must have flung it the night before. He opened the door to find Mark approaching, riding a horse and leading another.

"More cowboy training?" asked Charles.

"I don't know that I'd call this training. But I do know that nothing's better for a hangover than a ride in the fresh mountain air on a cool morning."

Mark stepped down from his horse and looped the reins loosely around the hitching post in front of the bunkhouse. He walked the other horse twenty feet away from the building then waved to Charles to come to him. "This is Sugar. She's a gentle old mare I keep around for kids and city slickers," he said with a smile as Charles approached.

"Don't be scared of her, she's kind of like your girlfriend, Suzanne. She's beyond her prime but still likes to be ridden," he said with a laugh as he patted the horse on the neck. Retrieving an apple from his coat pocket, he handed it to Charles and showed him how to feed it to her with a flat hand so Sugar didn't bite his fingers. Charles took the apple and fed it to the horse, then patted her like Mark had. The older cowboy showed Charles how to double check the cinch strap for correct tightness. He showed him how to pat every horse on the haunches before walking behind them so they didn't spook and kick. Then he instructed him how to mount the horse and stood back as Charles pulled himself up onto the saddle.

"Damn," said Mark. "Sitting up there, you almost look like a real cowboy!"

Charles laughed. He would give anything if Jodi could see him now. They rode up the lane behind the main house and eventually through a gate that Mark said was the easternmost boundary of his property. "I back up to almost two and a half million acres of Federal land, the Flathead National Forest. Not a bad neighbor."

As they rode up the trail, Mark gave the greenhorn tips from time to time. He told him to lean back a bit, to relax his shoulders, and let them sway with the motion of the horse's gait. They rode up the trail and then along an old logging road for almost an hour before Mark pulled up and stepped off his horse. He gave Charles instructions on how to dismount his horse without ending up on his butt. Then he showed him how to loop the reins around a tree branch.

Mark pulled some pine needles off a tree and crushed them between his fingers before smelling them. "It's been a dry summer. We could sure use some rain."

They walked around the area. Mark pointed out the difference between the Douglas fir trees that dominated the western slope and the different varieties of pines. He showed him the different needles, the bark, and the cones that helped identify each. He pointed out a Western Meadowlark, the Montana state bird, saying it was rare to see one this late in the season. Then he identified some other birds and squirrels they saw as they walked.

Charles said he was amazed at the amount of wildlife they saw. "The Flathead is home to deer, elk, beaver, wolverine, bobcat, coyote, grizzly bear, timber wolf, mountain goat, bald eagle, cougar, moose, and two species of fox," said Mark. "We've got it all, and I think over the years, I've seen just about all of them."

Something stirred inside of Charles. He felt something deep, again a strange, ancestral feeling. It was as if he was meant to be here. He felt like a cowboy who had been born and raised in the wrong place. He felt like he was home.

***

Jodi sat on the couch in her living room, curled up in a blanket. She had been there since before dawn, unable to sleep again. Her sleep was invaded by dreams and nightmares of Charles. He was just out of reach in the flames and the smoke, desperately reaching out to her, but she couldn't touch him. She woke in a sweat and decided that she would rather stay awake than chance the terror of another bad dream.

She cried, feeling guilty that she went out the night before and laughed with friends, then hugged another man while her husband's ashes lay somewhere in the rubble of his office building. She knew she couldn't spend another day buried in her guilt and her grief. She needed something to distract her on what would otherwise be a very long Sunday.

Outside her window, people seemed to be carrying on with their lives again. A family dressed in their best clothes walked to or from church. Mister Perkins, across the street, swept the stairs in front of his home. A woman walked by, her arms full of groceries while pulling a misbehaving toddler along behind her. Even her own mother had returned to Syracuse.

She knew she needed to get out then decided on a compromise. She hatched a plan that would get her out of the house and maybe offer her a little closure. She saw on the news that a memorial had appeared on the fence that had been built around the World Trade Center site. She decided it was time to see the rubble up close and to honor Charles by including him on the memorial.

With a plan in mind, she felt better. She felt more control in her life. She was making decisions rather than sitting idle and dwelling on her depression and her loss. She dressed, had some breakfast, and then searched through boxes of pictures until she found the right one. A picture of Charles, wearing a suit and tie. It was just after he had accepted the position with the Clark Financial Group and been given his office. She took his picture, standing in front of the office window, a view of the town he loved in the background.

Jodi held the picture while she admired how handsome he was, how sharply dressed he had been that day, and how proudly he smiled. He had been such a handsome man, she thought to herself. Realizing she had just used the past tense in her thoughts, she started to cry again. How could she be a widow at her age?

***

In church that morning, Jimmy White's thoughts were far away from the scriptures and the sermon. He thought of Jodi, Tinsley's pretty widow. And he thought of Vince DiPiero, a hothead who was already starting to act on his own. He was worried that if he didn't do something quickly, Vince was liable to grab her and then try to beat her husband's location out of her. White knew it wasn't beyond him to torture a woman. Vince was an animal.

Kidnapping and beating her might bring Tinsley out of hiding if he had any contact with his friends and family in Brooklyn. But if the guy was smart, nobody, including his wife and his family, knew he was alive. Normally, White wouldn't grab her unless he was certain that Tinsley would find out they had her. He had no reason to believe Tinsley would know they had her. But if he got to her before Vince, she might at the very least have a chance to die quickly and painlessly.

Death was an art form in White's mind. Anybody could beat the life out of a defenseless man with a baseball bat then dump his body in a back-alley dumpster. Not a single one of the people Jimmy White had killed during his career had ever been found. They simply vanished. It was a form of art, a skill that he had honed over the years.

In line for communion, he thought about her. He hated the thought of killing the woman, but he would be saving her from a painful, frightening death at the hands of Vince DiPiero. He felt it was the honorable thing to do.

During the final prayers, as the priest blessed the congregation and told them to "Go in peace to love and serve the Lord," Jimmy White was sketching a plan in his head. He needed a few days to get the little house in Hoboken ready and he needed to get the guys together. Tuesday night wouldn't work; he had a Knights of Columbus meeting. Wednesday would probably be best, if it fit into Joe's and Steve's schedules. He would meet with the DiPiero brothers to let them know the plan before Vince acted first. They needed a solid alibi in case they were ever questioned about her disappearance.

CHAPTER TEN

The two men on horseback followed the trail as it continued to climb the ridge. Sugar was a trail horse; she would follow the horse in front of her no matter where it went. Topping out at the ridge, Mark pulled up and stepped off his horse. Charles was in awe of the scene before him. Hungry Horse Reservoir lay below them, stretching to the north and south. On the other side of the reservoir, the mountains reached towards the sky, some of the peaks already sporting a dusting of snow.

"Wow," said Charles as he stepped down, gazing at the incredible view before him. "That is amazing."

Mark pointed out the Great Northern Mountains, Mount Grant towards the north, and Mount Cameahwait to the south of them. "Next spring, I'll take you around to the other side, up towards a little town called Essex. There's some high lakes in those mountains with some of the best fishing around."

Retrieving some trail mix and dried fruit from his saddlebags, Mark told Charles to grab the water bottles out of his bags and join him near the cliff's edge. Setting up the impromptu picnic on a stump, they enjoyed the incredible vista in silence for several minutes.

Charles broke the silence. "So, what's your story?" he asked without turning towards Mark

Mark gave him a glance. "What do you mean?"

"You can tell a lot about a man if you pay attention to the details," said Charles with a slight smile. "You've never talked about your past. You infer that you're from around here, but I hear Jersey in your voice. Your name is Irish, but you're clearly Italian. Trust me, I know the Italians. You carry a weapon with you everywhere you go. What's your story?"

Mark smiled. "I don't know that I have much of a story. I was raised in New Jersey, on the wrong side of Weehawken in a neighborhood that was torn down when they built the Lincoln Tunnel. My father was an Irish meat cutter, my mother was an Italian seamstress. In school, they called me McWop. Not a very flattering name, kind of like that Johnny Cash song, *A Boy Named Sue*. It made me tough and it made me mean, and by the time I was in high school, nobody called me anything but Mark. I knew from an early age that I wanted to get out of there. I always loved the old westerns, so as soon as I was old enough, I moved west to be a cowboy like Audie Murphy and Glenn Ford and Randolph Scott. I rode the train to Wyoming and got a job working for patient rancher who took me under his wing. He taught me to ride and shoot and fix fence. I guess that's why I hired you, a little payback to the karma gods."

That made Charles smile. He knew he wasn't getting the entire story—he might never learn it all—but he was happy to have somehow found the right cowboy on the right ranch.

***

It was a beautiful morning as Jodi stepped out of the brownstone and onto the street. Mr. Garver, a few doors down, gave her a wave as he carried a box up his stairs. The mean little kid from across the street stared at her while eating an apple that he probably stole from the corner bodega.

Walking towards the Metro station a few blocks over, she started to notice the world a little differently than she had the last two weeks. People were out; they laughed, they smiled. There were birds flying on the light breeze that blew up from the south. The world was starting to recover, so she needed to begin to recover. She was so enthralled with the activity around her that she didn't notice the man in the beige sedan parked on her block.

She rode the R-line onto Manhattan and got off at the City Hall station. When she arrived at the street level, she was shocked. Weeks after the attacks, the area around City Hall was still littered with paper and debris, and everything was coated with dust. As she walked south on Broadway, she started to see windows still broken by flying debris and gutters still clogged by dust and garbage. Turning west on Vesey Street, she walked past the closed and boarded up St. Paul's Church.

The fence surrounding the church had become an impromptu memorial and message board. She stopped to look at some of the hundreds of photos and notes. Half of them seemed to be messages of love. "Rest in Peace, Julia," or "Go with God, Martin." Others, put there by distressed friends and family, contained messages of desperation under the photos. "Missing, please call with any information."

At the corner of Church and Fulton, a chain link fence had been constructed to keep the curious away. The fence had also become a make-shift memorial. Flowers, stuffed animals, balloons, and photos had been placed by the thousands.

A woman about her age stood not far away, facing the fence. She leaned into the barrier, her head resting against the fence, obviously in tears. Jodi approached her and very uncharacteristically reached out to her, taking the stranger in her arms. She broke down in tears herself as the two women embraced each other. After several minutes, the other woman released her hug. She gave Jodi a warm, thankful smile as she wiped her tears, then without a word, the woman walked away.

Reaching inside her coat, she retrieved his photo. She put his picture and a flower on the chain link fence that surrounded that holy place in the ground. She looked at his picture on the barrier, then placed her head against it, like the woman before her, and cried.

***

As Charles and Mark returned on horseback to the Big Sky Ranch, Charles couldn't get Jodi out of his mind. He had to somehow tell her he was alive. He had to let her know of the better place he was in now. Contacting her by phone, mail, email, or even through a friend could put her life at risk. He swore at times he could feel her pain. He knew she must be suffering, knew she had to be grieving. He had to figure out some way to give her hope, to let her know that he might be alive without endangering her. Perhaps Mac Telford was the answer, he thought to himself.

They rode to the barn where Mark showed him how to pull the saddle and bridle. He gave Sugar a brushing, which she seemed to enjoy, then he gave her a couple of apples and a bucket of grain. "What's next?" he asked his boss.

"Well, it's Sunday, so why don't we take it easy today? You probably need a nap."

A nap sounded good to Charles. He headed towards the bunkhouse, but then had another idea. "Hey, Mark," he said while turning around. "I'm going to head into town for a few things. Do you need anything?"

Mark looked at the ground for a moment. "Can't think of a thing, but I'll think of something right after you pass through the front gate."

Charles smiled. He liked the old man. He couldn't think of a better place to be right now. He just wished Jodi was with him.

As he drove towards town, he changed plans and turned north on Highway 2 towards the town of Whitefish, about a half hour north, he guessed. He enjoyed the scenery of the valley on a gorgeous fall day. As he got closer to Whitefish, the farms and ranches gave way to development, more than he would have expected. Progress had made its way north. People drawn to the valley had moved to the area and built subdivisions and mini-malls where he guessed natural grasses used to sway.

Driving into Whitefish, he looked for a payphone in a quiet spot, away from the noise of the traffic. On Central Avenue, he instead found the Palace Bar and decided he needed a shot of courage before placing the call. The Palace had been a Whitefish standard for years. He stepped inside, and after his eyes adjusted, he found the interior to be just what he expected. Four pool tables stood in the back. A small group of guys sat around the bar visiting with each other, and a few others sat quietly with their beers.

He took a seat at the bar, two stools over from the one guy who didn't seem to fit. The man had the look of a tourist, although Charles couldn't put his finger on exactly why. He had a beer in front of him and worked feverishly on a piece of paper that he had written on and scratched out again and again.

After ordering a bourbon and water, Charles turned to the man and said, "You'll never get the words exactly right. Tell her if she was here, your actions would show your true feelings."

The stranger looked at him for a moment, a bit taken aback by his sudden intrusion into his deep thoughts. "Oh, it's not that kind of letter. I'm actually working on a song."

Charles smiled. "I figured as hard as you were working on that, that you were trying to convince a woman of something or apologize to her. I was going to get a copy of it when you were done, because I need to do the same thing. Right after I finish my drink."

The man smiled and reached towards him, shaking his hand. "I'm Jim."

"I'm Char...they call me Will," he said, catching himself.

The man smiled. In a soft southern accent, he explained, "I've got a little free time, so I thought I'd grab a drink and chat with some of the locals. That old guy sitting down at the end of the bar caught my imagination. I was trying to figure out line or two about a man drinking in a Whitefish bar. He'll tell you all the stories and show you all the scars. But I like the twist of a woman. I'll give that some thought."

"Do you write songs for a living?" asked Charles as the bartender sat his drink in front of him.

"Well, I'm trying to make a living at it," said Jim. "I spend most of my time in Southwest Florida, but I'm starting to build a small fan base up this way. I came up to play a couple of shows and then enjoy a few days of fishing."

Charles looked at the cocktail before him and laughed, saying to himself, "I wasn't gonna drink today." He shook his head then took a sip of his drink. "Well, good luck to you, both on the career and the fishing."

Jim held up his beer in a toast. "Good luck to you. Tell that lady you're trying to convince that she had better take advantage of the opportunity before her. You never know when the winds will begin to swirl and something mighty will take a right hand turn into your world."

Charles laughed. "I wish it was that easy."

"It never is," said Jim with a nod of the head.

***

Jodi was emotionally spent by the time she made it home. Her house had become her place of sanctuary, her little cocoon. It was her refuge from all stresses and strains the world seemed to throw at her since that morning Charles walked out the back door. She closed the blinds, threw her coat on the couch, locked the door, and curled up with a blanket in his chair. His smells were her most powerful reminder. At times, when she really needed him close to her, she would go into his closet and lie on the floor, just smelling his essence in the little room.

Her feelings bounced from one extreme to another. One moment she cursed God for taking her husband, the next she begged for his return. She often felt like she wanted to find a hole and crawl into it, then pull the dirt on top of her and never come out. Sometimes she felt like the answer was to start running and never stop. Uncertain what to do, she curled herself into a fetal position in his favorite wingback chair and buried her head under the blanket that still smelled a bit like him. She closed her eyes and tried to block out all the light.

***

After his shot of liquid courage, Charles walked across the street to a corner payphone and stared at it. Once he placed the call, there was no turning back. He had no idea of the level of sophistication available to the DiPiero brothers, or if they even thought he was alive. If they discovered he was alive, he didn't know their level of motivation to kill him. Would they just go after his wife? This one call could change his life and possibly end Jodi's.

Charles couldn't get her out of his mind. He couldn't imagine her pain and suffering, believing all this time he had died in his office. He didn't know if his disappearance would backfire on him. What if Jodi became angry and resentful at his charade? If she got beyond his desertion, there were still the years of lies he had told her. He hadn't actually lied to her; he simply hadn't ever mentioned that his biggest client was the infamous DiPiero family and that he laundered money for the mob.

He closed his eyes and tried to talk himself either into or out of the call he was about to make. Both decisions, making the call or walking away, had merit. Being stuck in the middle of the decision, standing on a street corner in Whitefish, couldn't go on forever. Finally, he reached into his pocket and pulled out some of the quarters he had gotten at the bar and started dropping them into the phone. He dialed the number, resisting the urge to hang up as it started to ring.

***

Walking home from church, Jimmy White placed a call to Joe Quintero. "Anything new?"

"Yeah. She left about nine fifteen and rode the Metro down to the World Trade Center. She left his picture and a flower on the fence down there, then got very emotional. Then she came back out to Brooklyn and went home. I just got back to my car a few minutes ago."

It sounded very normal, given her extraordinary circumstances. "Did she talk to anybody?"

"She gave another woman a hug. It looked like the woman was a widow too. They could have spoken or passed something. I wasn't very close to them," reported Quintero. "But I don't think they knew each other, if you want my opinion," he added.

"We're going to grab her on Wednesday night. Steve's getting the house ready. We'll work out some shifts."

"How long you gonna keep her?" Quintero asked.

"A couple of days, maybe up to a week," answered White. "If he doesn't flush out by then, he's not going to."

"Okay. Let me know," he said before he hung up the phone. Quintero shook his head. It was a shame to have to grab the woman. She seemed to him like an innocent pawn caught up in her pinhead husband's thieving business. She was so pretty, it was such a waste.

***

"Hello?" came the familiar voice on the other end of the phone. It was the first time in weeks that Charles had heard a friendly voice from his past.

"Are you in a position to speak freely?" asked Charles.

Mac Telford seldom answered his cell phone on the weekends; it seldom rang unless it was a client with an emergency. The voice on the other end of the line sounded familiar, but he wasn't sure who it might be. "I am," he replied.

"I assume the rules of attorney-client privilege still apply?" asked the voice on the other end of the line.

"Of course," replied Mac.

"Mac, it's Charles Tinsley."

Telford's eyes flew open wide. "Son of a bitch! I thought you were dead!"

"For all intents and purposes, let's just keep it that way. I don't need the FBI, the SEC, or the family to find out I'm alive."

"Where in the hell are you?" asked Mac.

"That, I can't tell you," said Charles.

"But you're okay? You got out of the building okay?"

"I wasn't in the building that day," said Charles. "I took the long way to work and everything happened before I got there."

The wheels started to turn in Mac's head as he reminded himself of the man's predicament. "Oh my God, Charles. Everybody thinks you're dead. You've got to find a hole, crawl into it, and never come out, ever!"

Charles breathed a sigh of relief. His plan had worked. "I'm already ahead of you. I've got a new life and a new place to live. Charles Tinsley will never reappear. But I've got to get Jodi out of there too. How is she?"

Mac shook his head, still amazed that he was speaking to a man he was convinced was dead until a few seconds ago. "She's taken it pretty hard. She thinks you're dead too. The SEC has frozen almost all of your assets. I got them to release your joint checking and savings accounts, and her law firm pitched in some money to help out, but she's not doing well."

Charles kicked the ground. "I need to talk to her."

"That's not going to be easy," said Mac. "My guess is that the FBI has a bug on your home phone and probably one on her office phone. The DiPiero family is probably watching her too. They may have bugged the house and the phones as well. Everybody is convinced you died but still operating under an abundance of caution since they haven't found a body."

Charles shook his head. "Is the FBI still in hot pursuit?"

"I think they're awfully distracted right now," said Mac. "They've got too much on their plates. They've lost interest in stock brokers and mobsters."

"Can you get Jodi away, alone, somewhere safe at ten tomorrow morning? I can call you back then."

"I can try," said Mac.

"Don't tell her anything," he begged. "I'll explain it all to her, and I'll let her know what she should do now."

Mac rubbed the back of his neck, already concocting a plan. "Yeah, call me at this number at ten tomorrow and I'll see what I can do." He paused for a second before saying, "You know you're going to have to handle this very carefully, on every side of the coin," the attorney warned.

"I know," replied Charles. "I know."

***

Sunday night dinner with the DiPiero brothers was predictable. As a power play, they arrived late. Vince wanted immediate answers, and Frankie was interested in results. They had chosen a small, family-owned Italian restaurant in the neighborhood. The food tasted like it was fresh out of a can and heated in a microwave. The wine was glorified grape juice, horrible. Huey sat at a nearby table trying to look tough, but it was easy to see that he was simply bored and wanted to be elsewhere.

"I've spoken with some of my contacts in the fire department," said White. "They don't think they will find any remains of those people in the North Tower between floors ninety-three and ninety-eight. There was simply too much jet fuel on the aircraft, and they believe the bodies were cremated to ash. Also, my associates in Chicago say Tinsley's BMW was sold to a chop shop there. It was dismantled, and the parts were shipped all over the country. We haven't been able to determine who sold the car to the chop shop yet, but we're working on it."

After taking a bite of his tepid plate of processed sauce over gelatinous ravioli, he continued. "I've decided to grab the wife," said Jimmy White. "My hope is that Tinsley will find out we have her and come out of hiding."

"Well, it's about fuckin' time that Little Jimmy Sunshine did something," said Vince in a sarcastic tone.

White calmly looked Vince in the eyes. "I'm forced to do something prematurely because you have been acting on your own. Sending Baby Huey to Chicago was a poorly conceived idea." Huey overheard the guy in the fancy suit use the nickname he disliked so much and sat up straight. "If Tinsley heard that you're looking for him, he may never reappear. Grabbing the wife will just be a desperate exercise in futility."

Vince was visibly shocked that White knew he had sent Huey to Chicago. "When you grab her, I'll come have a chat with her," said Vince with a smile. "She'll tell me where that pencil neck is hiding."

White removed his napkin from his lap, wiped the corners of his mouth, folded it, and placed it on the table next to his plate of Chef Boyardee's finest. "That's not going to happen. She doesn't know he's alive, or where he is. This morning, she was at the World Trade Center. She placed his picture and a flower on the fence, then cried uncontrollably. Beating her will not yield what she doesn't know."

Vince started to argue before Frankie raised his pointer finger, stopping his brother cold. White asked himself, *Where do I get a finger like that?*

"We won't interfere any further," said Frankie while looking at his brother.

Jimmy White stood. "It's your affair. I can help if needed, or I can step aside and let you handle it on your own. But I won't work alongside poorly conceived plans executed by an overweight, immature chauffeur."

Frankie got the message. "We won't get in your way again. Please let us know how we can help you."

Huey gave White a burning glare as he walked past him. Jimmy White smiled assuredly at the kid. He knew the youngster was worthless. White could tell by looking that, in a pinch, the kid would go for his gun rather than fight, even in the tight quarters of the small restaurant. If that fight was between the two of them, Huey would be on the floor with a broken kneecap and a busted jaw before he ever got a chance to wrestle the gun out from between his jacket and all the extra fat he carried.

***

Charles returned to the ranch just before sundown. He was hungry and tired and looking forward to a quiet evening. After making himself a simple dinner, he started a fire in the wood stove then glanced over the small selection of well-used paperback books on the little shelf in the corner. He selected a dog-eared Louis L'Amour novel. He had never read a L'Amour novel but thought he could pick up some tips from the classic western author that might help him look and act more like a real cowboy.

Sitting in the old recliner near the fire, he started reading L'Amour's novel *Conagher*, but after six pages, he fell asleep. He woke after an hour and set the book aside. A flicker out the window caught his attention. He could see a small fire burning in the yard out beyond the main house. Grabbing his coat and his hat, he walked out of the bunk house, down the stairs, and towards the fire.

Mark sat alone at the campfire on a round of firewood. "Mind if I join you?" asked Charles.

"You're always welcome to join my fire," said Mark. "I even brought an extra glass just in case you did," he said as he held up his glass of whiskey.

As Charles sat on a log next to him, Mark poured three fingers of whiskey into a tumbler and handed it to him. They didn't talk for a long time. They sat and enjoyed the crackle of the fire, the far-off call of a coyote, and the beauty of the Montana moon as it slowly rose over the mountains. Below them, to the west, they could see the distant lights of town, but it felt as if they were a million miles removed from the people down there.

"On a clear, moonless night," Mark finally said, "there are so many stars that it will almost frighten you."

"I've hear the term 'God's Country' before, but I never knew it existed until I arrived in this valley," said Charles quietly.

Mark reached over and clinked his glass against Charles' in a silent affirmation.

"I need a few hours tomorrow morning to finish up some personal business," said Charles. "I won't make a habit of it."

Mark quietly nodded.

Charles took a large sip of his drink and felt the burn in his throat as the whiskey went down. "There's something I need to tell you. Something I've been meaning to tell you. You've been more than fair with me; I need to be honest with you."

"What's that?" replied Mark.

"I have a lot of baggage, a lot of trouble back home," admitted Charles. Mark looked at him, showing the young man he had his full attention, but said nothing. "I was a financial advisor. My biggest client was a mob family in New Jersey. I got greedy, they got greedy, I got involved in some transactions that made me and the family a lot of money before the SEC got wind of it. They tipped off the FBI, and when they arrested me, I turned on the family to try to keep my butt out of prison."

Mark swirled the whiskey in his glass while looking back at the fire. "Well, that had to piss them off."

"Yeah, they have a contract out on my head. And, since I left town without testifying, I'm sure the FBI is after me too."

"You're right," said Mark. "You've got a shitload of trouble back home."

"My saving grace," said Charles after a few moments of silence, "is that everybody thinks I was in my office on the ninety-fourth floor of the World Trade Center when it got hit. The best I can tell, if I was at my desk, I would have died from blunt force trauma with a 767."

Mark raised his eyebrows. "Everybody?"

"Everybody, until today. I called my attorney this afternoon. I have to let my wife know I'm alive. I can't let her keep thinking I died. He's going to get her somewhere tomorrow morning that I can talk with her safely."

After finishing his drink in a big swig, Mark poured more from the bottle and swirled it by the fire. "Which family?"

"The DiPiero family," Charles answered. He thought he saw a slight twist of Mark's head at the mention of the name, but it might have just been his imagination. "Have you heard of them?"

"Everybody from Jersey's heard of the DiPiero family. The old man was a mean bastard. I heard the sons are a couple of idiots."

Charles laughed. "They are idiots, but they're idiots with guns, and if they had a chance, I'm sure they would like some revenge."

"The FBI thinks you died?" asked Mark.

"I think so. My attorney said they got very quiet after the terrorist attacks."

"I'm sure they got their hands full," said Mark. "Maybe you'll get lucky and your case will get buried under a huge pile of bureaucracy." Mark leaned forward and put his elbows on his knees. He seemed to be contemplating the situation. After several minutes, he sat back, saying, "I can't have the FBI snooping around here, for reasons I don't care to discuss. If they ever discover you're in the area, you're going to have to leave. The DiPiero boys don't bother me. I wouldn't mind if they showed up here one day."

"I don't want to put you at risk," said Charles. "I'll leave tomorrow."

"Hell," said Mark as he picked up a stick to stir the fire. "You're safer here than you are out wandering around the countryside. And surprisingly, you're a pretty hard worker for a city prick."

Charles finished his whiskey and stared into the fire. Something about this strange place felt familiar. It felt safe and comfortable.

CHAPTER ELEVEN

"Who are the flowers from?" asked Melissa, the woman whose desk sat across from Jodi's.

"I don't know," replied Jodi as she arrived at her desk at the start of the work week. She removed her coat, set down her backpack, and opened the card. It read, *"I'm ALWAYS here for you. Your hugging buddy."* Jodi knew immediately who had sent the flowers.

She blushed, just a little, but Melissa picked up on it. Her coworker decided not to tease her, knowing the emotional rollercoaster her life had become. It was okay that she had an admirer; anything positive right now, anything that put a little life into Jodi's soul was okay with Melissa. But she was dying to know the identity of the mystery man.

Jodi folded the card and put it in her pocket. "They're from my mom," she lied.

"Right," replied Melissa in a sarcastic tone.

***

Mac Telford made a mental note to give his assistant a raise. Her 1977 Volkswagen Rabbit was a pile of garbage. He should have borrowed someone else's car. Mac had no reason to believe that anybody was watching him, but he was sure that either the family or the FBI, and maybe both, would be keeping an eye on Jodi Tinsley. He didn't want to try to get her out of her office in his Mercedes.

He drove the twenty-four-year-old car out to Brooklyn, remembering to feather the gas at stoplights to keep it from dying. After parking in the underground garage at her building, he rode the elevator to the eleventh floor. He handed his business card to the receptionist, explaining that he was her attorney, then he asked if she could go get Jodi rather than calling her. The young lady seemed a little put out by the strange request but agreed to walk back to get her.

"Hi, Mac," she said when she returned with the receptionist.

"Do you have someplace private we can talk?" asked Mac.

Jodi pointed to a conference room just off the reception area and said, "Sure, we can go in here."

Mac followed her in and closed the door behind him. "I need you to take a ride with me. I need about an hour of your time."

"Right now?" she asked.

"Yeah, right now, please."

Based on the look on his face and the tone of his voice, Jodi didn't ask any questions. "Let me get my coat and tell my boss I'm leaving."

"Please don't use your desk phone," he said. "It might be bugged."

Jodi gave him a curious look then left to get her coat. On her way back to her desk she stopped by Eric's office. "Thank you for the flowers," she said with a smile.

"I don't know what you're talking about," he replied with a wink.

"My attorney is here. He needs to meet with me for an hour or so. I can stay late."

Eric smiled. "Take whatever time you need. I'm staying late too." *The later the better,* he thought to himself.

***

Charles felt reasonably safe calling Mac Telford's cell phone. The FBI was probably able to intercept and trace cell phone calls, but the DiPiero brothers didn't likely have access to such technology. He assumed that the FBI might have their home phone and perhaps Jodi's office phone bugged, but they probably didn't go so far as to bug Mac's cell phone. He only drove as far as the Lucky Pick Casino, about three miles from the ranch, on the corner of Highway 35 and Lake Blaine Road. At the payphone outside the building, he called Mac at the time they had agreed.

His mouth was dry, his knees were weak. Everything was riding on this phone call. His entire life hung in the balance.

***

On the elevator ride to the underground parking garage, Jodi asked Mac what his strange visit was all about. Mac could only ask her to be patient. In the old Volkswagen, he handed her a scarf and a pair of cheap sunglasses and asked her to wear them. He put on sunglasses and a baseball cap himself. They drove in a haphazard route for five minutes, making multiple turns while Mac watched for a tail.

Feeling confident that they weren't being followed, he turned into a three-story parking garage and had just made it to the roof level when his cell phone rang. "Hello?"

"Hi, Mac, it's me," said the voice on the other end of the line. "Do you have her?"

"She's here," said Mac then he handed the phone to Jodi.

Jodi took the phone from him with a questioning look on her face. She cautiously put the phone to her ear and said, "Hello."

Mac pulled into a parking spot near the stairs that also offered him a view of other cars coming up the ramp. He turned off the engine and looked at Jodi. Her face was twisted in a look of disbelief and shock. Her hands started shaking as her face turned an ashen color. She turned her head slowly to look at Mac with a strange, inquisitive look right before the phone slipped from her hand and fell between the car's front seats, then she fainted.

Digging for his cell phone with one hand while reaching for her face with the other, he patted her cheek, saying, "Jodi, are you okay? Jodi?"

On the other end of the line, Charles had heard her voice. It was just one word, but he knew it was her. It was the voice he had been dying to hear for weeks. He forgot every word of his rehearsed speech and said, "Jodi, it's Chas. I'm okay and I love you." He had waited for a response, but getting none, he started to tell her that he hadn't been in the building, when he heard a loud clunking sound, then the distant voice of Mac saying her name over and over.

Charles listened intently, calling out to Mac and Jodi over muffled sounds of a voice, clunks, and bangs. Finally, after fifteen or twenty seconds that seemed like an eternity, he heard Mac's voice on the other end of the line. "Are you still there?"

"I'm here. What the hell happened?" asked Charles.

"She fainted," said Mac. "Hang on a second."

He heard Mac talking, and he thought he heard her voice respond. Charles pressed the receiver against his ear so hard it hurt as he plugged the other ear with his finger to drown out the sound of the wind.

He could hear the muffled tone of a conversation but couldn't hear the words. One voice was Mac's and one, he was certain, was Jodi's. After several minutes, he heard Mac ask, "Are you okay? Are you sure?"

Then he heard her voice weakly on the phone, "Chas?"

"I'm here, Jode. It's me."

"Are you okay? Where are you?" she asked, her voice faltering. She was obviously in tears.

"I'm okay," he replied. "I wasn't in the building that morning. I can't tell you where I am, but I can tell you that I'm safe."

Mac quietly asked her if she was okay. She nodded, then he slipped out of the car to allow them some privacy. He stood about fifteen feet away from the car, leaning against the railing. For twenty minutes, he watched as her emotions changed from sobbing uncontrollably to anger. She was obviously giving her husband a verbal tongue-lashing. Eventually, her emotions seemed to calm, and she almost looked like she was conducting business. Finally, in the minutes before the call ended, she seemed to be expressing her love to him. She returned to tears, but they were different, soft tears rather than the sobbing from earlier.

When the call ended, she looked around to see where Mac had gone. She got out of the car and walked to him, surprising him with a long and warm, silent hug.

***

With the exception of Jodi fainting, the call had gone reasonably close to what Charles had imagined. In less than twenty minutes, their conversation had gone from her shock, to disbelief, to anger, and finally, to acceptance. He knew she would be stunned to learn he was alive. He had hoped that once she got over the astonishment, she would get to excitement and joy, but she turned to anger quicker than he had expected.

She scolded him for his actions, both his business dealings and his decision to leave her believing he was dead. She tried, but she couldn't help expressing her love for him between her bouts of anger. Before the end of their call, he was able to get her to agree to listen to his excuses for his actions at some future point in time as he apologized to her over and over. He told her he was working on a plan to get them together again soon, but she needed to be patient and to continue to act like a grieving widow.

After agreeing to talk again the following Sunday, the emotions overtook them both. They spent the last several minutes of the conversation in tears, expressing their love and devotion to the other. "I promised to stay with you through good times and bad," said Jodi. "I'll stick to my end of the bargain, but that doesn't mean I won't give you a black eye the next time I see you."

That made Charles smile. He knew he deserved at least a smack on the face for what he had put her through, all because of greed. Driving back to the ranch, he couldn't help but roll down the window and feel the coolness of a crisp Montana morning on his face. They had a thousand difficult conversations ahead of them, but Jodi had told him that she loved him and that was all that mattered at that moment.

Mark had just finished his conversation and hung up the phone, when he saw his ranch hand's truck coming up the lane. It hadn't taken long to confirm what Charles had told him. The FBI in New York had set aside non-critical cases to focus on the terrorist attacks. His connection at the Bureau, a paper-pushing buddy from his childhood, was able to quickly locate the case and report its status to Mark. At the moment, the justice system couldn't give a damn about the DiPiero brothers and their financial advisor, a young guy named Charles Tinsley.

Pouring the last of the coffee into his cup, he put on his coat and hat then walked out to the porch. He stopped and took a sip of the hot cup while watching Charles walk towards him. "How did your phone call go?" Mark asked. He could tell from the smile that it must have been good.

Charles stopped at the bottom of the stairs. "It went well. But as I'm sure you know, in business and love, the first reaction isn't always the true reaction. We'll talk next weekend. That might be a difficult conversation once she's had time to think it over and really let her anger loose."

Mark smiled. "You're a pretty smart guy for a dumb-ass stock broker who got tied up with the wrong clients."

Smiling, Charles said, "Last night, you called me a city prick; today, I'm a dumb-ass stock broker. Are you trying to piss me off?"

After taking a sip of his coffee, Mark replied, "I just call them as I see them."

"I like that about you," said Charles. "What's the plan today?"

Mark tossed the bottom of his coffee out across the yard. "I'm going to show you how to saddle Sugar one more time, then I want you to go up and start looking at the eastern section of fence. You go down to the little shop, there's several coils of barbed wire. Grab one and the old saddle bags I sat next to them. The bags have your cutters, a fence stretcher, a hammer, and the tacks you'll need when you get up there."

Charles shook his head. "I can saddle Sugar and get the wire and saddlebags. I just need you to show me how you want me to mend the fence when I find a problem."

The older cowboy smiled at the young man's independence. "Okay, I'll meet you down at the corral in fifteen minutes."

***

"What was that all about?" asked Melissa as Jodi took off her coat and started to log in to her computer. One look and she could tell the meeting had been significant. Jodi's face was flushed, and she looked distracted and out of breath, almost glassy-eyed.

Jodi lied, "He wanted to talk over the procedures for declaration of death without a body. It might help me with some life insurance we have. He wanted to get me out of the office in case I got emotional."

Melissa didn't buy the story. The conversation Jodi had described wouldn't have the urgency that the receptionist described coming from the attorney. "Why did that conversation have to take place out of the office and without an appointment?" she asked.

Jodi shook her head. "Mac's a strange guy. He's a great attorney, but you never know when he's going to show up and need to discuss something." She logged on to her computer and tried to look busy. She didn't want to lie about the meeting to Melissa anymore.

She wanted to scream to the world that he was alive, but she understood the importance of the FBI and the mob believing he was dead. She wanted to tell somebody, to share her emotions. For a brief moment, she considered leading Melissa to the restroom to tell her the news, but she knew she couldn't.

Her mind spun in circles. Sitting at her desk, staring at her computer screen, Jodi tried to put her emotions in some sense of order. Charles was alive. She was, at the same time, mad as hell at him for what he had put her through the last few weeks and incredibly joyful that he was alive. She wanted to hug and kiss him while repeatedly punching him.

He would only tell her that he was a long way from New York, and that he was safe. He instructed her not to tell anybody he was alive, not even her mother. He told her the phones in their house and her office probably weren't safe. He even warned her that the Feds or the mob might have placed bugs around their home. Anything she said could put the two of them in jeopardy.

When she asked him how long he had been dealing with the mob, he truthfully answered, "My entire career." Charles assured her that life was over. He said he was excited to show her his new life. He was eager to show her a place that was so incredibly different from what they were used to, a place so enveloped in beauty that it would astound her. He had professed his love for her over and over, and he had convinced her that the most important thing in the world was for them to be together soon.

She believed him. She would be happy living in a little shack with nothing but his love. She wanted nothing more than to be with him, but she wasn't able to tell him that she was pregnant.

***

Jimmy White walked around the little house in Hoboken for the first time in months. The older gentleman he had hired to keep it up was doing a fantastic job. The tiny yard was nicely trimmed, the white picket fence had a new coat of paint. The flower beds had recently received their fall cleaning and were ready for the coming winter.

He had purchased the home under the name of a deceased homeless man to use for his work. Over the years, the little idyllic nineteen-twenties clapboard house with the white fence and grandmother-looking drapes had been the site of some nasty dealings with some horrible people. Stuck in the middle of a quiet neighborhood, it was the perfect home for his needs. The garage was off the alley, a short twenty feet from the back door, which led to stairs up the home, and down to the concrete-floored basement. Insulation in the ceiling and boarded-up windows made the basement a nearly soundproof vault.

After checking the outside of the home and chatting briefly with the elderly man sitting on his porch next door, White entered through the front door. The main floor of the house was clean and well kept. The furniture looked like an older couple had lived there. The two small bedrooms were ready for him and his men with fresh sheets. The single bathroom had fresh towels.

In the kitchen, the refrigerator had been stocked as he directed. There was plenty of food in the cupboards for a week. He double checked the supply of coffee and was happy to find a new, unopened can of Folgers above the coffee maker.

The basement was clean. A single chair sat alone above a drain in the middle of the concrete floor. A small cot was pushed up against one wall. Other than a few boxes of items he had requested that sat on the tiny workbench in the corner, the dimly lit basement was empty.

Confident the home was ready for its next guest, he left through the front door, nodded to the neighbor, and drove away in his nondescript Oldsmobile.

CHAPTER TWELVE

Sugar was patient as Charles struggled with the bridle. She stood still as he fumbled with the blanket and wrestled with the saddle. Mark had been waiting several minutes, when Charles finally led her out of the barn and into the corral.

"Hitch her over there and I'll teach you everything I know about mending barbed wire." In ten minutes, on a stretch of fence just beyond the corral, Mark taught him how to loop and fix a broken stretch of wire using the fence stretcher. He showed him the correct tension, how to fix a post, and how to tack wire back to the post.

He spent another twenty minutes watching his hand do the tasks under his supervision. Mark was impressed. The guy fumbled, he hooked his jeans in the barbed wire several times, and nearly lost an eye when the strand of wire sprang back at his face, but he didn't lack in his enthusiasm to learn.

Walking back over to Sugar, Mark showed him how to attach the coil of wire to the saddle so he didn't scratch the horse or himself. Then he grabbed the reins as Charles got ready to mount the horse. Mark should have pointed out the mistake to the greenhorn, but he always figured the fastest way to learn was to fail a few times.

Charles got his boot up into the stirrup then grabbed the saddle horn. As he pulled himself up, the saddle slipped off the horse's back and down Sugar's near side, spooking her and dropping Charles on his butt in the dirt next to her.

Mark busted out laughing at Charles lying in the dust while trying to calm the horse at the same time. "You knew that was going to happen," said Charles.

"Yeah." He chuckled as he held the reins tightly, saying, "Easy girl." He instructed Charles to move around to the other side of the horse and release the saddle. "Sugar gets pretty excited when she thinks she's going to go out for a ride. She tends to puff up her chest a bit. You always need to check the cinch strap on her before you mount her."

"Thanks for the tip, jackass," said Charles as he loosened the strap.

"I figure the best way to teach a slicker how to ride is to let him to fail a few times." Mark laughed. "You'll never make that mistake again, right? Come over here and I'll show you how to cinch that strap correctly. Then we'll straighten out the bridle and tie on this Pulaski."

After getting the rig on Sugar straightened out, Mark pointed Charles in the right direction, towards the eastern fence line, and told him to be back well before sundown. "The last thing I need to be doing is searching for a lost city prick up there in the dark. You won't get to it all today. You'll be up there again tomorrow morning."

***

Much to her boss's surprise, Jodi didn't stay late as she had promised. Instead, she left early. Eric had tried to visit with her in the mid-afternoon to discuss a case brief she had been writing, but it was clear that her mind was a million miles away. She seemed to have problems forming a simple sentence, her eyes were glassy, and she was very distracted. When he asked, she simply said she had a lot to think about after talking with her attorney earlier in the day. He didn't press her for more information, hoping she would open up to him more when they were alone in the office together after hours.

Her early departure had derailed his plans. He had imagined them working late, then before she had a chance to leave, he would casually sit on corner of her desk and ask, with a mirror-practiced look of concern, how she was doing. After she opened her heart to him, he would offer her a hug of support then suggest they get a bite to eat at the little French café a few blocks away. There, they would enjoy a little too much wine over a late dinner.

Something the attorney had said had thwarted his plans. He was sure it was just a temporary setback. Tomorrow, he would spring a "critical" project on her in the late afternoon. They would have to work late to complete it, and then he would suggest the café down the street. It was just a minor delay in his long-term plan.

Joe Quintero was also surprised when he saw her leaving the office at least an hour early. The moment he saw her, he felt like something had changed. She walked with a little spring in her step. He had followed her a half dozen times and had never seen her walk with her head up, her shoulders back, and a hint of a smile on her face. Jimmy White had told him about the potential fling with her boss. He wondered if there was a new development in that relationship or if she had heard something about her husband. He watched her walk to the corner and get on the city bus, then he started his car and followed the bus to her stop. She stepped off the bus and walked to her brownstone with the same springy stride. Something had changed.

Quintero parked then dialed Jimmy White's number.

***

It had been a long half day of work. Charles was beat as he rode back towards the barn. The eastern fence was the highest and most remote border of the Big Sky Ranch. Much of it was on steep terrain that had been cleared of trees and brush when the current fence was built. Now that section was overgrown with tangles of brush, and some of the fence was crossed by fallen trees.

The Pulaski tool Mark had sent along was a favorite of the Forest Service, developed not far from the ranch in 1911 by a Forest Service employee, Ed Pulaski. It was a combination hand tool with a mattock on one side of the head for digging, and an ax on the other side for chopping. Using the tool, he cleared brush and cut away small trees for hours. He cleared and mended one section of fence before attacking the next. The work was back-breaking, and the barb wire tried to cut every piece of exposed skin it could find. He sweated and cussed, and realized he was having the time of his life.

During breaks, he had thought about Jodi with a smile. It had been so wonderful to hear her voice. Even when she was angry at him, he reveled, knowing she was there on the other end of the phone. He knew if he could get her out of New York safely, they might have months of struggles, talking through the years of deceit and slowly rebuilding her trust in him. But he imagined them together, somewhere out here in the mountains of Montana. It would be worth the struggles and the wait.

Mark walked out onto the porch with a coffee cup in his hand as Charles rode past the house. "How'd you do?"

"The brush is pretty thick, and there's a lot of trees down, across the fence," said Charles as he leaned on the saddle horn.

After taking a sip of his coffee, Mark said, "I wonder if I gave you more of a task than one man can handle. I'll ride up there tomorrow after breakfast with a chainsaw and have a look."

Charles gave a nod and rode towards the barn. He wanted some dinner, a shower, and his bunk. Something about Mark's statement bothered him as he pulled the saddle from Sugar. It was a huge job, and he knew his boss likely hadn't surveyed the scope of the task, but Charles didn't want help. He had been given a job to do and he wanted to complete it himself. In his heart, he knew he needed to complete eastern section alone, but he also knew there were trees too big, too large up there to handle with just an ax. He didn't know a thing about operating a chainsaw. He knew he needed some help, but his pride didn't want to admit it.

***

There was a lot going on in her head, but the one emotion that overruled all the rest was one of immense relief. She was so angry with Charles for his business dealings and the problems they had created. She was furious at him for leaving and not trusting her to be a part of the plan. But above all that, beyond the anger, the frustration, and the fear she was experiencing, she felt elation that the only man that she had ever truly loved was alive. She wanted to dance in the rain, she wanted to shout from the rooftop, and more than anything else, she wanted to hold him, kiss him, and tell him, face to face, that she loved him.

He had shared with her that he was working on a plan, but she had to be patient. It might take months to put the pieces in place to allow them to be together again. She had told him about the finances, that the SEC had seized most of their assets, and she worried about keeping their home and her inability to make the payments on her tiny income.

"They are going to take the brownstone," he told her. "They'll take our investment accounts and sell everything they can get their hands on under the guise of restitution to the investors that they think I cheated. Those investors all understood the risks involved with investing in startup companies and penny stocks."

He told her what Mac and her mother had told her, to quit making payments on the home loan. He told her she would be out of there before the bank ever had a chance to foreclose.

Jodi walked around her home and looked at their beautiful things. She thought about the life she had in Brooklyn, her career, her friends, his family. She thought about the implications of picking up and leaving it all. She hadn't considered losing every possession she owned, everything she had bought, collected, or been given over the course of her life. But when she had time to look at the artwork, the furniture, and their other belongings, she realized they didn't mean a thing to her. Charles was her life; everything else was fluff.

For now, she would play the part of a grieving widow. She would go to work, then come home and lay low until he shared the plan he was hatching. She wouldn't tell a soul he was alive, not even her mother. It wasn't going to be easy, but it was what she had to do if she planned to spend the rest of her life with the man she loved.

***

Convinced Jodi was in for the night, Joe Quintero drove into the city to meet with Jimmy White. Over a cocktail at a little bar in Hell's Kitchen, he told his boss, "Something's changed. She's acting differently."

"In what way?" asked White.

"It's hard to describe. It's like the black cloud that's been hanging over her head since I started tailing her is gone."

White ran his fingers through his thinning hair while thinking. "Maybe the fling with her boss is a real thing. She doesn't seem like the type to jump into something serious so soon, but stranger things have happened when a spouse dies." He tilted his head to the side. "Or maybe, she somehow found out her husband is alive."

He sipped on his drink while looking out the window as he thought about Jodi Tinsley. "I'll follow her in the morning," he told Quintero. "I'll see if I have the same impressions as you. This could change our plans. We might want to grab her Tuesday night rather than Wednesday if we think she's been in contact with her husband."

"Is the house ready to go?" asked Quintero.

"Yeah."

"And we'll dispose of the body the usual way?" he asked.

"Yeah," said White quietly.

***

Charles was up and out the door before sunrise. The cold autumn winds swept down from the Salish Mountain Range, blowing east across the Flathead Valley. The weather was certainly starting to change. Shivering, he pulled up the collar of his jacket as he walked to the barn. He saddled Sugar under a single lightbulb above the first stall outside the tack room. After tying on the saddlebags and the barb wire coils, he led the old horse out to the corral. Reaching for the saddle horn, he remembered the previous day's lesson and stopped to tighten the cinch strap before mounting the horse.

Charles rode out past the still dark main house and up the back lane into the timber as the eastern sky lightened. As he made his way to the towards the top of the ranch, he stopped at a point and looked out across the valley. The sun was just cresting above the eastern slope enough to light the very top of the mountain peaks to the west of the valley. It was breathtaking.

Sugar shook then bowed her head, seemingly asking him if they were going to waste the entire day standing around looking at the sunrise. Charles pulled the reins slightly to the right and gave her a tap with his heel, and the horse turned and started up the trail.

Jodi would never believe the transformation he was making without seeing it for herself. He couldn't have imagined he could make it as a hand ranching and riding the fence line at dawn. In no time, the number-crunching, paper-pushing, white collar city boy was gone. He never wanted to return to that life. Charles had found where he was supposed to be and what he was supposed to be doing.

After clearing brush and fallen trees for more than an hour, he turned at a noise below him to see Mark riding up the trail leading a pack horse. "You cleared all this by yourself?"

Charles looked back at the progress he had made. It didn't look like a lot to him in terms of distance, but it represented a lot of hard work. "Yeah, I cleared it all. Is there another way to do it?"

Mark stepped down from his horse and looped the reins around a fence post before leading the packhorse up towards Charles. He tied the lead to a small tree then pulled a small chainsaw from the pack before walking to the other side and removing a second, much larger saw. "Ever use one of these?" he asked as he carried the two saws up to his hand.

"Nope," said Charles.

"Well, they will do the work of ten men if you use them correctly. Unfortunately, they were designed to maim their user. You need to always pay attention because they will try to cut your leg off. They will try to kickback and ruin that pretty face, and if they can't hurt you themselves, they will encourage the brush and the trees to try to snap back and get you."

"I think I'll just stick to the Pulaski," said Charles.

Mark laughed. "I'll show you how to use the small one to clear brush while I use the big saw to take out the larger trees. You'll get the hang of it pretty quickly."

One thing Charles had come to appreciate about Mark in his short time on the ranch was his easy way of teaching. If he hadn't been a teacher or instructor in his previous life, he had missed his calling.

Mark showed Charles the different parts of the saw. He told him how it worked and then how to start the saw, then showed him. He showed him how to hold and use the little chainsaw safely and what to watch for when cutting so the brush didn't snap back towards him. Then he stood back and watched while Charles started and used the small saw to cut small limbs and brush.

Once confident in his hand's ability to safely use his saw, Mark picked up the big saw and went to work on some of the larger trees across the fence line ahead of them. After an hour, Mark hiked back down to where Charles was pulling brush he had cut away from the fence. "Let's take a break. I brought a thermos of coffee and some biscuits I made a couple of days ago."

As they sat on a pair of stumps, Charles devoured the biscuits while sipping on the hot coffee. After a bit, Mark looked up. "So, Mister Wall Street, how are you at picking solid investments in a crazy market like this one?"

The answer rolled off his lips before Charles could catch himself. "It depends on what your goal is. If you want security, the utilities stocks are always a safe bet. People need water, electricity, and gas no matter what the economy is doing. But if you want some big gains, there are a number of opportunities available. Big gains come with increased risk, however."

Mark smiled. "We'll have to talk more. I have a chunk of change sitting in CDs right now that isn't doing me much good."

Charles realized he had broken character, something he would have to be careful about in the future. In a slow western drawl, he answered, "I'm not sure what you're talkin' about. I'm just a Montana saddle bum."

"Then grab those coils and let's get that last section of fence up. Then we'll tackle that steep stretch up there," said Mark.

***

Jimmy White wasn't sure he could detect a difference in her mannerisms. He stood under his umbrella at her bus stop a few blocks from Jodi's home and watched her approach. He got on her bus and sat a few rows behind her. She stared out the window as they made their way towards her office. Approaching the stop, he stood and got off the bus before her, turning away from the direction of her building but then turning to follow her after a few seconds. He didn't see what Quintero had described; she didn't appear to be skipping to work with an ear-to-ear smile on her face. But it was a rainy, gloomy morning, so nobody was skipping or smiling.

At the entrance to her office, she met another woman coming from the other direction. There, White saw something. They hugged under the portico, and Jodi smiled and laughed as they shook out their umbrellas. He was too far away to hear the words. It appeared the woman had asked Jodi how she was doing. Jodi's answer, and her smile, seemed to speak volumes.

Crossing the street, White ducked into a little coffee shop for a warm cup of coffee and a scone. Something had changed. He needed to find out what, and he only had one other resource up his sleeve.

Eric Mills had noticed something too. In the meeting with Croft & Ellis, a water rights firm from Nevada, Jodi seemed more upbeat. She took an active role, answering questions, offering suggestions, even making a joke while seemingly shaking off the depression that had been her norm for the last few weeks. When the meeting ended, she gave each of the attorneys from the visiting firm her card, she smiled, and told them to call her with any questions. She encouraged them to use her as a resource in the case they were pursuing. It was the old Jodi, the pre-September 11th Jodi.

After the group from Croft & Ellis had left, Mills gathered his group for the always important meeting after the meeting to debrief. There, she was a completely different person. She joked with her co-workers and smiled. She was the brightest star in the room, thought Mills.

Leaving that meeting, Eric said, "Jodi, can I see you in my office for a moment?"

"Sure," she said then followed him to his office.

After closing his door, he smiled, saying, "Wow, you are in a good mood today."

She smiled while looking at the floor. "I've been in such a bad place for so long. I need to smile again, and I need to laugh again. It's always going to be hard, but at some point, I need to be me again."

Eric was more captivated by her beautiful smile than ever before. "I'm so glad to hear that. I know you have a long road ahead of you, but attitude is everything and yours is incredible. Hey, I need to get the Santa Clara County allocations brief done and out to them tonight. I was hoping you could stay a little later and help me. I'll buy you dinner if you can help out."

Jodi saw through the ruse; she knew that brief wasn't due for weeks. Eric was a nice guy, and if Charles had actually died, she might have eventually gone out with him. But her heart belonged to her husband, despite his lies and his absence. "I'm so sorry, Eric. I have plans this evening. I didn't think that brief was due for several weeks. If I had known it was due tomorrow, I would have had it completed and on your desk days ago."

Mills shrugged it off and told her he would get it done. After she left, he sat and wondered what had changed. Since the previous day's meeting with her attorney, she had acted completely different.

His thoughts were interrupted by a phone call. "Eric Mills," he said into the receiver.

"Mister Mills, my name is Ron Verhei. Do you have a moment?"

"Of course, Mister Verhei. What can I do for you?"

"I am Jodi Tinsley's uncle, on her mother's side," said the man on the other end of the phone. "I understand that Jodi is one of your direct employees."

"She is," replied Mills. "She's one of my best."

"Jodi's mother and I don't talk anymore. Family dynamics; I'm sure you understand," said Verhei.

"Certainly," said Mills.

"My wife and I think the world of Jodi. She is one of our favorite nieces, but given the bad blood in our family, we don't feel like we can contact her. We are dying to know how she is doing, with her husband's situation in the Trade Center mess."

Verhei's voice told it all. Eric could tell he was a kind and concerned uncle. "It's been a hard couple of weeks for her," he told the man. "She's struggled a lot, but we've tried to be there to support her. I've tried to be there to help however I can. Today, she seems like a new person," he continued.

"Why is that?" asked Verhei.

"I'm not sure," said Mills. "I asked her, and she told me she needed to laugh and smile again. I know she met with her attorney yesterday, something he said to her, some advice he gave to her? I don't know, but she's a different person than I've seen in weeks. She seems like herself again."

"That's wonderful to hear," said Verhei. "May I ask for two more favors?"

"Sure," said Mills.

"May I call you from time to time to check up on her, and could you keep our conversations completely discreet? I don't need to muddy the family waters any further, especially given the situation. I'm sure you understand."

"We never had this conversation," said Mills. "Please feel free to reach out to me at any time."

"Thank you, Mister Mills. You are a saint," said Verhei before he hung up.

Eric Mills hung up the phone feeling pretty good about himself. Getting in good with the family, even the rogue side of the family, couldn't hurt.

Across the street from Jodi's office building, Jimmy White ended the call with Mills and set his cell phone on the coffee shop table. Jodi met with her attorney and everything had changed, he thought to himself. It was time to check out the attorney.

CHAPTER THIRTEEN

"Did you bring some lunch up with you?" Mark asked around noon.

"I brought some stuff; leftover bacon, some apples, a bag of chips," said Charles, thinking of the items he had hastily stuffed in a duffle bag.

"It's a damn good thing you work for a guy like me. I brought a bunch of leftovers. We'll have to eat it cold because I couldn't find an extension cord long enough to reach up here, and I couldn't figure out how to pack the microwave on the back of the mule. That's the other thing."

They shared what they each had while sipping on two cans of Coke that Mark had brought along. When they had finished eating, Mark stood and walked to his horse, where he pulled a rifle out of the scabbard. "I brought along a .22. It's easier on the ears and easier on the wallet for target shooting." He handed Charles the gun then reminded him to always check the safety when he picked up a gun or when somebody handed him one.

Walking down the fence line, he set his half empty Coke can on a few stumps about forty yards away then set a small flat rock on top of it. After getting back up to where Charles sat, he reached out and took the gun from him. "This is a Ruger 10/22, probably the best built, most dependable weapon you can buy for under a hundred and fifty bucks." He reached into his pocket and pulled out a bullet, then handed it to Charles. "It shoots like a .22 long rifle, good for targets and squirrels but not much else."

He showed him how to cock the rifle, sliding a shell into the chamber. Then he handed him the gun and told him to take a shot at the Coke can. Charles carefully took aim, leaned forward just a bit, then let his breath out, like Mark had shown him. He squeezed the trigger, and nothing happened. Mark smiled. "It will make a little more noise with the safety off," he said with a laugh.

Charles lowered the gun. "You love watching me make mistakes."

"It's a new hobby of mine," he said with a chuckle.

Charles pulled the gun back to his shoulder, turned off the safety, took a breath, and fired a shot. The can didn't move. He was surprised by the lack of kickback and the almost comically quiet report from the rifle. The only guns he had fired were Mark's Winchester rifle and his big Glock .45

"Nice shot," said Mark sarcastically. "Now try to hit the big red can down there." Charles took careful aim and fired again, but the can stayed put on the stump.

"What's wrong with this thing?" Charles asked.

"There's nothing wrong with the gun. It's operator error," Mark said with a laugh. "Try again, Mister Magoo."

On the sixth shot, the can fell off the stump. "Geez, finally," said Charles. "I'll go set it back up." When he got down to the stump, he picked up the soda can. It had five holes in the front side and five in the back. He walked it back up to Mark, who was impressed. The stockbroker hit the can five out of six times. His steady hand and good eyesight made him a natural. They took turns shooting at random targets. After they emptied and reloaded the ten-round magazine a few times, Mark finally said, "Let's get back to work. It's gets dark early these days. And I'm getting tired of getting out shot by a rookie."

***

Jimmy White was on his phone in the café, gathering what information he could about Jodi's attorney, a man named Mac Telford, when he saw her leave the building with another woman. He started to gather his things to follow them, but they stopped less than a half a block down at a hot dog vendor's cart. From his vantage point, he watched the two attractive ladies playfully tease the older man who ran the cart. The three seemed to know each other. They probably had lunch at the cart a couple of times a week because of its convenient location.

After the man served them, they stood a few feet away and continued to joke with the man, even as he helped other customers. Jodi's face seemed to glow; she had the face of a happy woman. A strange twinge of jealousy caught White off guard. He planned to spend some time with Jodi soon, but he didn't believe, even for a moment, that she would joke and laugh with him.

When they finished their dogs, the vendor seemed to show them some sort of trick with a coin, which made them both laugh. They each gave the man a quick hug and walked back to the office. White couldn't help but agree with Joe Quintero's assessment. Something had changed.

His inquiries into Mac Telford yielded nothing out of the ordinary. Telford worked for a medium-sized Midtown law firm. He didn't seem to specialize in anything, one of thousands of general counsels in the city. White picked up the phone and called Telford, using the Uncle Verhei ruse to see what information he could gather. The call went completely different from his call with Jodi's boss. Telford told him he was unable to disclose any information about any client and that he wouldn't confirm if this Jodi Tinsley person was or wasn't his client.

White used his best acting skills to try to persuade the attorney to offer some tidbit on how Jodi was doing given the situation, but Telford kept giving the same answers. "I'm sorry, I can't divulge any information about anybody without their consent."

After the call with "Uncle Verhei," Mac called Melissa, the woman whose desk was near Jodi's. He asked her to put Jodi on the line. "Jodi, it's me. Don't say my name. I just received a call from your Uncle Verhei. He wanted to know how you were doing, but I can't give him any information without your permission."

"Who?" asked Jodi.

"He said his name was Ron Verhei, your uncle on your mother's side."

Jodi shook her head. "My mother's maiden name is Shervik. She only has one brother, Jim. I don't have an Uncle Ron. And I don't think I am related to anybody named Verhei."

"I'm glad I didn't fall for it," he told her. "It was probably a reporter trying to get some information on a victim's family, or it was the mob." A chill ran down his spine. "I think the FBI would take a more direct approach. I'm not sure how a reporter would know that I represented Charles," he told her as he thought through the strange call.

"You need to be very careful about anything you say over your office phone and probably your home phone too. They might have your house bugged as well. Anything you say inside your house may be heard by somebody else."

Jodi felt violated. It didn't matter if it was the FBI or the mob that was listening. It was just creepy to think that somebody might hear her shower, dress, or even snore. "Can you think of anything you've said on either phone over the last couple of days that might lead somebody to me?" asked Mac.

"I can't think of a thing," she said as Melissa listened with great interest to the one-sided conversation. "I talk with my mom almost every night, but I'm very careful not to mention anything to her."

"Okay. I'll look into it more from my end, but please be very careful. Somebody is fishing for information about you."

"I promise, I'll be cautious," she said before hanging up the phone. She explained to Melissa that some reporter had called, trying to get information out of her attorney. It was probably somebody looking for a new angle to report on the victims' families.

"Scumbags," replied Melissa.

As she sat at her desk, Jodi tried to remember every conversation with her mother over the past few days, since she spoke with Charles. She couldn't recall a single thing that she said that might have put their secret in jeopardy. She thought about her chats with other friends, with Melissa. She had been so careful not to say anything.

The only piece of personal information she could remember discussing over her office phone was the appointment she had made with Doctor Christensen, an obstetrician.

***

Shutting down his saw, Mark yelled up to Charles, "Let's knock off for the day. I'm beat." Charles gave a wave then completed the repair splice on the section of wire he worked.

As Charles made his way down the hill to Mark and the horses, he yelled, "When do I get to fix fence on flat land?"

Mark laughed. "Don't worry, we've got plenty of fence on the lower section that needs fixing too." He had just finished securing his saw to the mule, when Charles handed him the smaller saw.

"It's getting cold," said Charles.

"Yeah," replied Mark. "They say there's a chance of snow by morning. That's why I wanted to get up here and help you today. Looks like we need about one more day to finish the east side, then we can start working down the south line. That drops down to level ground pretty quickly."

"Will the snow stay, once it falls?" asked Charles.

"Not this time of year. In the fall and spring around here, we always say, 'If you don't like the weather today, just wait for tomorrow.' It can drop six inches of snow tomorrow and be seventy degrees the next day."

After securing the gear, Charles mounted up and waited for Mark to pass him on the thin trail down the mountain. They had gone just a few hundred yards, when Mark heard a loud "whoomph" behind him. He looked back to see Charles lying on the ground, his saddle hanging from Sugar's belly. The horse stood still, not spooked this time by the strange feeling of the dangling saddle and the rider below her.

Mark burst out with a huge belly laugh as he watched Charles struggle up from the ground. "Just when I think you're going to make a pretty good hand, you decide to take a nap under your horse!"

"Screw you," Charles replied as he got up from the ground while rubbing a new bruise on his butt.

***

Laura King had the most unique job of anybody she knew. She spent eight to ten hours a day analyzing recorded conversations. She was given access to recordings and told key phrases and names to listen for, but she was also asked to listen for anything out of the ordinary. She didn't completely understand the legality of listening to the recordings and she didn't know that most of them were obtained illegally. Laura wasn't even sure who sent them to her, but she had become good at picking out and reporting the pertinent conversations to whoever employed her. She had developed skills, learning quickly what was relevant and what was not.

The boring part of her job was listening to the recordings from inside a home or office, those picked up by a hook switch bypass. A hook switch bypass, when installed, made every phone receiver in the house a microphone, even when they were on the hook. There was often silence followed by a brief conversation, followed by hours of listening to somebody rustle around their home. A program on her computer helped; she could fast forward through much of it, only listening to sounds that were above a certain decibel level. But if the subject was watching TV, listening to music, or vacuuming, for instance, she would have to listen to make sure they didn't say something significant.

Phone conversations were easier. With years of experience, she could tell in seconds if the conversation was noteworthy. People seemed to talk differently when they had something to say that nobody else was supposed to hear.

The paralegal in the law office, one of the people she was monitoring for a nameless client, had made and received numerous phone calls. The lady, Jodi, had a nice voice, and she seemed likeable. Several people had offered her condolences. Laura quickly picked up that her husband was one of the victims of the World Trade Center attacks. Laura was surprised and a little saddened when she heard Jodi make an appointment with a doctor, saying she thought she was pregnant. It was such a shame, Laura thought, thinking of all the children who had lost their mothers or fathers in the senseless attacks.

She noted the appointment in the log that she would forward to a vague AOL email address.

***

Jimmy White needed to stop. He needed to slow down, take a breath, and think about what he was doing. Calling the attorney, Telford, had likely backfired. The attorney probably called Jodi to ask about Uncle Verhei, only to find out that it was a made-up name. He was planning to grab the woman and sit on her for a week or so, hoping Tinsley would come forward. He pinned all of his hope on the guy hearing from her friends or relatives that she was missing. The local media might pick up the news of her disappearance, but Tinsley would need to be in the New York area and see it on the evening news or read it in the newspaper. It was all pretty weak. He felt like the DiPiero brothers were forcing him down a path that he knew better than to follow.

Sitting in his den, he closed his eyes and tried to organize all the pieces. If Tinsley was in hiding, he might be in Chicago, but that might have just been a jumping-off spot. He could be anywhere in the world by this point. The sudden mood swing in the wife led him to believe that she somehow recently found out that he was alive. They may have even spoken. Her perspective on life, based solely on what he had observed and what her boss had surrendered, seemed to go from hopeless to hopeful in a very short period of time.

As he was trying to decide on his next move, the familiar computer-generated male voice said, "You've got mail!" He opened his eyes and looked. It was from an email address he recognized as the service he employed to listen to Jodi's recordings. He honestly didn't know if the person was male or female, but it didn't really matter. Whoever they were, they had proven themselves to be the best he had ever worked with. They reported conversations that couldn't seem relevant to anybody unfamiliar with the subjects, but dialog that changed the course of people's lives.

Glancing through the email, the listener reported a phone call at 10:32am to a Doctor Christensen's office. Jodi asked for an appointment, telling the receptionist that she thought she was pregnant.

White leaned back in his chair, closed his eyes, and said out loud, "Son of a bitch."

***

After a simple dinner, Mark Mulligan relaxed in his easy chair with a book. He pulled a quilt over his knees, knowing he would likely fall asleep reading. He had just started the fifth chapter of a new Tom Clancy novel, when he thought he heard a shot outside. He didn't jump up; it sounded like a .22, and only a single shot. He listened for a moment, then went back to his novel. A few seconds later, he heard another shot, followed by another after that. Standing, he walked to the window and cautiously looked out.

Down near the irrigation berm, a single lantern illuminated about twenty beer cans sitting on an old log. Charles knelt on the porch of the bunkhouse, using the rail as a rest, and fired in the dark at the cans with the Ruger. Mark watched as he fired eight more shots, hitting cans on all but the last. The guy had a talent for shooting, and he seemed to like it. He must enjoy it; the outside temperature had fallen below freezing. Retreating to his book, his chair, and his quilt, he heard about a hundred more shots with pauses that were obviously reload and target reset periods. The gun finally went silent about the time Mark fell asleep with the novel on his chest.

Charles couldn't feel his fingers when he finally decided to go inside to the hot fire he had built in the woodstove. Shooting was easy and fun. He would have to ask Mark how he might get a few of his own guns, given that he couldn't go down to the local gun shop and fill out a registration form to buy one. After warming up, he walked down to the berm with a grocery sack to pick up the hole-filled empties and retrieve the lantern. A light snow began to fall as he walked back up to the bunkhouse. He couldn't wait to see what the valley looked like blanketed with snow.

***

Morals were a tremendous handicap in his profession, but Jimmy White knew he couldn't proceed. He couldn't grab and eventually kill an innocent pregnant woman. And in reality, it no longer made sense to grab her. If she was somehow communicating with her husband, the pregnancy alone might bring him out in the open. Tinsley might make the mistake that White had been hoping for and reveal his whereabouts. White's morals didn't extend to Tinsley. Given the chance, he'd kill the stockbroker, pregnant wife or not.

He lay awake at 3:00am, trying to figure out how he was going to convince Vince DiPiero to be patient. The correct move was to wait a few weeks for Tinsley or his wife to screw up. Convincing Vince of that was going to be difficult. If he wasn't able to get the DiPiero brothers to wait, he would be forced to grab the girl before Vince had the chance. Her death, either way, would be on his conscience, but at least in his hands, it would be a pleasant passing. He lay there thinking of the life ahead of her. Killing her was a waste, and even with all of his precautions and planning, kidnapping and murdering somebody always involved risks.

Perhaps he could get Frankie to buy into his new plan first. Frankie had always been the voice of reason between the two brothers. If he could convince Frankie to be patient, then perhaps Frankie could convince his irrational and excessively spontaneous younger brother to relax and let the scenario play out.

Strangely, Jimmy White could never recall meeting with just one brother. They were always together for their meetings. He would call Frankie in the morning to see if he could meet with him alone. It might backfire, but the risk was worth the reward.

By 7:30am, Jimmy had showered, shaved, and dressed. He placed the call. Frankie answered on the second ring. "Frankie, it's Jimmy. Have you had breakfast?"

"Not yet," said Frankie.

"Let go get some eggs, just you and me. You know that little hole-in-the-wall place on 45th, off Broadway, Maria's or Mary's or something like that?"

"Yeah, they make a good omelet there," said Frankie. "I'll meet you there in about a half an hour."

Traffic at that hour of the morning was a mess, so Frankie beat him to the restaurant. While White was happy to see him sitting in a booth alone, he wasn't so happy to see that Frankie had taken the "gunfighter's seat." Jimmy was a cautious man. He liked to sit with his back against the wall, facing the door, where he had a view of anybody who was coming near him. He wouldn't have that luxury at this meeting.

"Sorry I'm late," Jimmy said to Frankie as he wiggled into the vinyl-covered booth.

Frankie waved off his tardiness. "What's on your mind, Jimmy?"

"There's been some developments," he said as the waitress poured him a cup of coffee. He waited until she was out of earshot before continuing. "We've noticed a sudden change in the wife's mood. She seems happier, almost like she's heard some good news. Maybe she's heard from Tinsley. We're not sure, but something has lightened her mood. And we think she's pregnant. I'd like to wait it out a few weeks to see if the kid screws up and comes out of hiding."

Frankie took a sip of his coffee while thinking it over. "A change in her mood is pretty thin to go on. Maybe she's just happy to be pregnant?"

"I have a hard time thinking any woman would be overjoyed to bring a baby into the world when she just lost her husband," replied White.

"You know as well as I do how nuts women get when they got a bun in the oven," said Frankie with a snicker. "What else you got?"

"I spoke with her boss, and he said the same thing. He thought something changed too, right after she met with her attorney."

"Who's the attorney?" asked Frankie.

"A guy in Midtown, Mac Telford," said White. He grimaced right after saying the attorney's name. He couldn't believe he had slipped.

"So she met with this Telford fella, and suddenly she's happy?" asked Frankie.

"Well," said Jimmy, trying to cover up his mistake. "It was within a day or so after she met with him that we started noticing a change. I'm not sure if that meeting had anything to do with it or not. I'd like to lie back for a week or two to see what happens. I'll bet Tinsley screws up soon."

"I don't know, Jimmy. If we grab the wife, the guy's gonna come forward, right?"

"Maybe," said White. "If he's really in communication with her or anybody near her. But if we're wrong, if he really is hiding out there somewhere and hasn't been talking to anybody, he may not know we have her. Then we've taken a lot of risks and a lot of lives for no reward. I'd have no reservations with the plan if we were certain she was chatting with the guy, but we just don't know."

Frankie sipped his coffee while he thought about the options. He silently asked himself what his old man would have done. His father, Markus DiPiero, was the toughest guy he ever knew. Every kid grew up thinking their father was a mean, tough son of a bitch, but Frankie's father was the real deal. He ruled Jersey with an iron fist and was a shoot first and ask questions later sort of guy. But the old man also had a soft heart for the innocent and defenseless people in the world. What would the old man do in this situation?

"Okay, Jimmy. We'll lay off the girl for a couple of weeks. The FBI is so busy chasing terrorists right now that they seemed to have forgotten about us. That won't last forever, but we got some time to go with your plan."

White breathed a quiet sigh of relief. "Thank you, Frankie. We'll keep following her, we'll keep listening. But you've got to control Vince. He can't be running around acting on his own. If we give it some time, I'm convinced Tinsley will turn up."

CHAPTER FOURTEEN

Charles was surprised when he woke and saw daylight coming through the windows of the bunkhouse. Except for his hungover morning, he had always awakened before dawn. He climbed out of his bunk and walked to the woodstove, where he tossed two pieces of firewood on top of the white coals. He closed the stove's door and opened the dampers, and a moment later heard the satisfying sound of the wood catching fire.

Out the window, he could see the snow-covered barn roof. Grabbing the blanket off his bunk, he wrapped it around him and stepped to the window. The scene before him was amazing. Snow was nothing new to him, Brooklyn was blanketed in snow every year; sometimes several feet of snow covered the familiar streets around his neighborhood. But here, it was magical. The pine trees below the barn held several inches of snow on their bows, each looking like his mother's flocked Christmas trees from his youth. The dirt- and mud-covered barnyard and corrals were white and clean. Everywhere, the ground looked freshly painted.

As he looked across the valley, the scene was surreal. The brilliant white snow made everything look clean and uniform. The rising sun to the east, behind him, was just starting to shine on the tops of the peaks on the far side of the valley. They glowed in an almost golden color. He had never witnessed such amazing natural beauty.

A hundred yards away, Charles could see Mark Mulligan standing motionless on the porch of the main house. He might have never noticed him if he hadn't taken a drink of his coffee, creating a motion that caught his eye. The man stood, staring out across his land, the valley, and the towering mountains beyond, seemingly in awe of the beauty before him.

Charles was intrigued by the man on the distant porch. He was tough, a no-nonsense sort of man with seemingly little time for anything but work. But after spending a little time with him, Charles found he enjoyed their conversations. Mark seemed to find enjoyment in teaching Charles what he knew: how to ride, shoot, fix fence, and even drive a manual transmission. And Mark seemed to take a little time out of each day to enjoy the beauty that surrounded him. Mark was a man with many layers, and Charles suspected, a man with many secrets in his past.

Suspecting that Mark had extra coffee, and not wanting to wait for his own to brew, Charles pulled on his clothes and stomped into his boots before walking over to the main house. Mark seemed to be happy to see him coming up on the porch and went inside to grab two fresh cups. They stood in silence and looked over the amazing scenery of the distant snow-covered Flathead Valley that stretched to the west. The sun had reached the far side of the valley. Charles watched as the shadows from the mountains behind him quickly shrank.

"I was planning more heavy work today," Mark said after a long silence.

"Yeah?" answered Charles.

"Yeah. Thought we'd restack the last of that old alfalfa upfront in the pole barn so we can use it up before spring. We can use the frontend loader for some of it, but a bunch of it's just going to be heavy lifting."

Charles nodded then said, "Had breakfast?" Mark slowly shook his head from side to side. "How about I go put some eggs on? We can tackle that project with a full stomach. And over breakfast, I need some advice from you," he added.

Mark smiled. "I was hoping you'd get around to asking my advice. Yes, that hat looks stupid on you."

Charles looked at him. "What? No, that's not what I was going to ask. Wait, does this hat really look stupid?"

"It's nothing a little shaping won't fix. Hell, I might even be able to do it over the tea kettle in the kitchen," said Mark with a laugh. "You go get cooking, I'll be over in a few minutes."

Charles walked through the two or three inches of snow back to the bunkhouse, where he stomped off his feet on the porch before going in. He stopped and looked at himself in the mirror near the door. "I don't think my hat looks stupid," he said out loud as he admired himself in his secondhand cowboy hat.

He hung his coat on a hook, started a pot of coffee, then dug through the refrigerator until he found the leftover bacon. He tossed that in a skillet then started cutting up some onion and red pepper, which he put in another pan with some vegetable oil. On a whim, he started cleaning some potatoes to dice and fry.

By the time Mark stomped off his boots on the porch, Charles had a feast underway. "Good lord, boy. I thought you were going to cook some eggs. How can I help?"

After the potatoes were cut and in the pan, Mark sat down at the table and hung his hat on the chair next to him. Charles flipped the bacon in the pan then turned around. "I need to get my wife out of New York, but I'm not sure how to do that without tipping off the FBI and the DiPiero brothers. I only get one chance and screwing it up could get her killed."

"Yeah," said Mark quietly. After a moment, he looked up like he had an idea. "Is that coffee ready?" Charles dropped his head slightly in disappointment. He grabbed the pot and filled a cup before handing it to him.

"How are you communicating with her?" Mark asked after a sip.

"I call my attorney on his cell phone from a random payphone at a specific time. He makes sure she is away from the office or our home. Last time, she was in a parking lot in a car he had borrowed."

Mark looked up. "I'm glad you're being careful. I can give you my cell phone number; it's got a Louisiana area code. She can call here from a cell phone or a payphone there. Never let her call you from the home or office phone, any usual phone they might bug." He took another sip while thinking. "Slipping her out of town is fairly easy, like a magic trick. You make sure everybody is looking at the right hand while she slips out to the left. Sort of like the trick you unintentionally pulled off. Everybody was watching the towers fall, then you slipped out of town while their backs were turned."

"That sounds easy," said Charles.

"How hot are things in New York?" asked Mark.

"I don't really know. I've heard the FBI is completely distracted by terrorists at the moment. My guess is that the DiPiero boys are willing to be as patient as they need to be, just so long as I end up dead."

"Are you and your wife willing to disappear forever? You'll need fake IDs, fake social security numbers, assumed names, and you'll have to live that way for the rest of your lives." said Mark.

"I know I am, as long as she's with me."

Mark rubbed his chin. "It sounds easy, but it's a different life. Before you make any move, you need to make sure she's willing to live the remainder of her life based on lies. Contact with your friends and family is nearly impossible. Making new friends is risky."

Charles said what he had suspected for a few weeks. "It sounds like you have some experience with that type of life."

"I don't know what you're talking about," said the old cowboy.

***

While Jimmy White was calling off the planned kidnapping, Frankie was having a very difficult conversation with his little brother.

"I've said it a thousand times, you're too soft for this business, Frankie," said Vince.

"And like I told you," replied Frankie, "this isn't our father's business anymore. We can get more done with brains than with muscle these days. We're not a bunch of thugs running around the alleys collecting protection money from shopkeepers. We're a ten-million-dollar-a-year corporation with diverse investments and multiple income streams."

Vince shook his head in frustration. "You take care of the diverse investments and income streams. I'll make sure nobody stops the money coming in or tries to take what we got."

"Lay off the woman for a couple of weeks. Let Jimmy handle this," said Frankie in a firm, fatherly tone.

"We're just wasting time and money with that fancy-dressed piss ant while Tinsley slips farther and farther away. If you'd let me handle it, he'd be dead by now."

Frankie was frustrated too, but not with Jimmy White. He knew that allowing a professional handle the situation added a layer of protection for the family. Jimmy White also got things accomplished without the cloud of revenge that blinded Vince. Frankie knew that if Tinsley appeared on the street in front of a hundred police officers, his overly emotional brother would kill him right in front of them.

He needed something to distract Vince. That was when he remembered the attorney. "Listen, do me a favor. Jimmy White mentioned that Tinsley's wife met with his attorney, a guy named Mac Telford. He works for some Midtown firm. Can you quietly check him out?"

Vince looked down at the table between them. "Now you want me to do Jimmy White's job? Check out a Midtown attorney? Yeah, I'll check him out."

Frankie cautioned him. "Just check around, see what he knows and who knows him. He might be another piece to the puzzle or he might not know anything. We don't want to cross him, and we don't want to tip him off that we're onto him."

"Sure, Frankie, I'll check him out, nice and quiet," said Vince with a malicious smile.

***

Sunday couldn't come quick enough for either of them. Jodi put on a nice dress and enjoyed the walk to Saint Augustine's church, just a few blocks away. Mac, dressed in disguise, beat her there, arriving thirty minutes before mass started. He sat in a pew in the middle of the church and legitimately prayed while waiting for her. When the attractive Mrs. Tinsley sat in the pew next to him, he slid his cell phone towards her, which she slipped into her purse. Ten minutes after mass started, she slipped away to the ladies' room.

Charles was up. He had finished breakfast, washed the dishes, and waited impatiently for the right time to call. In the empty bunkhouse, using Mark's cell phone, he pre-dialed Mac's number and waited for the clock to indicate the correct time, then hit the green "send" button.

The phone had barely rung, when he heard her voice. "Chas?"

"Hi, Jode, how are you?" he asked.

"I'm good. I miss you so much. How are you?" she asked.

"I'm fine, and I miss you too. More than I can tell you," he said. "Do you have a piece of paper? I want you to write down this number. You can call it. You'll probably have to leave a message, but you can call it any time from a safe location. Don't ever call it from your office or our house, okay?"

"Okay," she said as she dug through her purse for a slip of paper and a pen.

After he gave her the number and asked her to read it back to him, he said, "Listen, Jode, more than anything else, I want us to be together somewhere safe."

"Me too," said Jodi as she wiped a tear from her eye.

"That means leaving everything, forever," he said.

"I know," replied Jodi.

"We might not be able to see your mother again, at least for several years. We won't be able to contact my family, or our friends," he told her. "We'll have a new life in this beautiful place I've found. It's an amazing place, but it's completely different from anything you're used to, completely different."

"As long as you're there, as long as we're safe, I don't care where we go," she said. He believed her.

"I'm putting together a plan. It might take several months, maybe even until spring," he said. "I need to get you out of there in a way that throws everybody way off your track. I need them to look the other direction while you sneak off behind their backs," he said, paraphrasing Mark. "They will never know where you went. We'll change our names and change our lives. We'll be safe and happy together in one of the most incredible spots on earth."

"Spring is so far away," she said.

"I know it is," he replied. "But I need time to make sure all the pieces and parts are in place so they never find us. They won't even know where to look. Are you a hundred percent sure you're willing to give up everything?"

Jodi thought about his question for a second or two. "I would be giving up everything if I didn't come to you. I won't be leaving behind anything that really matters."

"I'm so excited for you to see this place," said Charles. "I had seen pictures of it, but until you're here, you can't imagine the beauty. I have a job doing something crazy, something I had never even remotely considered, and I'm loving every moment. It's like I was born in the wrong place. I should have been born here."

Jodi could hear the excitement in his voice. She couldn't wait to see the place he described. They agreed on a call schedule, professed their love to each other, then ended the call. Jodi slinked back into the pew next to the man with the disheveled hair and dark glasses. She slid his phone back over to him and tried to focus on the sermon.

Six rows back, Jimmy White returned to his pew. After trailing her to the restroom, he could only hear a muffled conversation while discreetly standing outside the door. She had been speaking with somebody. He ducked inside the men's room when he heard her heels walking towards the door across the tile floor of the restroom. She obviously had a cell phone. The only logical conclusion to this bathroom charade was that she had just had a conversation with her husband.

He needed to figure out how to tap into a cellular conversation. He knew a guy who might be able to help him.

In the back row of the church, Kelly McGuire was trying to figure out what the attorney was doing. McGuire had worked for the DiPiero brothers for years. It was never a surprise when Vince called and asked him to do something unusual. For a few days, he had been tailing an attorney.

The guy had acted very normal until McGuire saw him leave the parking garage on Sunday morning. He followed the guy across the East River to a church in Brooklyn. He was surprised when the Midtown attorney got out of his Mercedes. He was dressed in old jeans and a hooded sweatshirt. His normally well-kept hair was messy, and he wore dark glasses. It was an obvious attempt at a disguise and he might have gotten away with it if he hadn't left the building in his own car.

In church, the attorney sat alone in a middle pew. When mass was over, he returned to his car without speaking to or making contact with anybody. If he passed a note to someone, it must have been during the offering of peace, when the congregation turned and shook hands with those around them as a sign of peace. He noted the young family in front of them, the Hispanic couple behind him, and a pretty woman in the pew next to him.

The attorney drove directly back to his Midtown apartment building. McGuire made notes of his movements, the possible contacts, and the way he was dressed. He'd report to Vince later in the day.

***

In Jersey City, Vince DiPiero sat at the table in his kitchen over a cup of coffee and a bowl of oatmeal. None of his contacts had ever heard of this attorney, Telford. He had tried to be smart, like Frankie had asked. He had him tailed, he checked with multiple people trying to find some information on the guy. After several days, all he knew was public information. The guy was married, lived in a comfortable apartment in the city, and belonged to a few prestigious clubs. He had never stepped out of line with the law and he didn't seem to have any skeletons in his closet.

Frustrated with the investigative approach, he was ready to take a more direct tactic. He picked up the phone and called Kelly McGuire. After learning that the attorney had donned a disguise and drove to a church near Tinsley's home, Vince was very suspicious. Vince quickly convinced himself that the attorney was helping facilitate communication between Tinsley and his wife.

Vince wasn't the brightest bulb on the string, but even he could put one and one together from Kelly McGuire's report. The attorney had gone to a church in Brooklyn, just blocks from Tinsley's home. He sat alone in the church, trying to disguise himself, seemingly only having contact once with a couple, a family, and a pretty woman, a strawberry blonde in her late twenties. The cloak and dagger act was enough to convince Vince that the guy was trying to pull something. He was ready to have a chat with the attorney.

***

Jodi was elated after talking to Charles. She wanted to share her joy with everybody, wanting to skip home from church, but remembered the warning from both Mac and Charles. People might be watching. She needed to continue to play the part of the grieving widow.

Leaving the church, Jodi noticed a well-dressed man who look familiar, but she couldn't think where she knew him. They briefly made eye contact before he quickly turned away. A block from her home, she stepped into the corner bodega to grab a few items. A chill ran down her spine when the same man from church walked past the store heading towards her home. She hurried to the window to watch him. He stopped at the corner, looking up and down the street, as if he was looking for someone, maybe her. She ducked back into the store out of his sight. "Shit," she said, trying to convince herself she was just being paranoid.

After purchasing her items, Jodi ducked out of the store and quickly walked in the opposite direction. She turned down the alley behind the brownstone and entered her house through the backdoor. She spent the rest of the day hiding in her home, peeking out the windows looking for anything unusual, jumping at every odd sound.

By the end of the day, she hadn't noticed any suspicious figures watching her from the shadows on the street. She shook her head and told herself she was just being silly. Nobody was after her. She slept fitfully, waking several times to check that the doors were still locked. When morning came, she was still alone, still alive, and still tired. She showered, dressed, and acted as normal as possible as she made her way to work along her usual route. She didn't notice anything or anybody who seemed out of place, and she didn't see the man from church again. As she settled into her desk, Joe Quintero settled into the café across the street for coffee and his second breakfast of the morning.

***

Mark had been right. After the back-breaking work on the eastern stretch of fence, with the steep terrain, fallen timber, and overgrown brush, the work on the relatively flat southern fence line was easy. Charles worked alone, riding the fence line, fixing posts or wire where needed. He had become pretty quick at fixing a broken stretch. It wasn't difficult: make a loop at the end of each of the broken ends by bending the wire back on itself before securing it with four or five twists. Then he would insert the wire stretcher, ratchet the line tight, and insert a section of new wire. Every now and then, he would stop to take advantage of the view of the mountains or the valley. His office was the most incredible place he could imagine.

During one of his short breaks, he wondered if Jodi would embrace his newfound lifestyle and the Flathead Valley with his same excitement. She loved the beach, the tropics, and often talked about going back to Key West or other places that were warm and sandy. He couldn't remember her ever talking about wanting to go to the mountains to ride horses and chase cattle. He loved the life he was adopting, he loved the mountains and the valley, but he loved his wife more than all that. He decided that if she didn't fall in love with the country life, he'd take her somewhere south. He would trade his second-hand cowboy boots and hat for shorts and flipflops in a heartbeat as long as Jodi was happy.

The only thing he wasn't willing to do for his beautiful wife was to go back to a lifestyle that required a suit and tie. Standing next to a barbed wire fence that brisk morning, he promised himself that he would never again wear a tie. He would remember to tell Jodi that when he died, hopefully in sixty or seventy years, to not lay him out in a coffin with a suit and a tie. That life was gone. He would never again put a corporate noose around his neck or wear an office straitjacket. He'd be a cowboy, or a beach bum, or whatever his wife wanted him to be. But he'd never be a businessman or an executive again.

CHAPTER FIFTEEN

Kelly McGuire hadn't watched Mac Telford enough to establish any of his patterns. Vince DiPiero wasn't patient enough to wait for patterns to be observed or for a plan to be formulated. They wouldn't have the luxury of catching the attorney in a quiet place where they were unlikely to be seen abducting him. Vince's plan was to simply find an opportunity to push him into a car with stolen license plates as he walked home from his office. Then they would drive to one of the family's warehouses in Jersey, where they could have some privacy. McGuire believed the attorney's fate was in his own hands. Vince knew otherwise.

Vince and Kelly found a parking spot on the street, next to a Thai restaurant along Telford's most likely walking route from his office to his apartment. As they sat in the gray Chevy sedan, they talked about sports and politics, Vince commented on the "caboose" of the pretty young lady who walked by. Kelly was slightly taken aback by the normality of the conversation; it was as if they were waiting for a bus on the street corner. It was as if what they were about to do was normal to Vince.

"Here he comes," said Vince, seeing the gray-haired man wearing an overcoat and carrying a briefcase walking towards them. "You open the back door like you're getting something out of there," said DiPiero.

As Vince got out of the car as the man approached their parking spot, Kelly couldn't believe they were really going to do this on a busy sidewalk. Walking towards the restaurant, Vince acted like he didn't see Telford, nearly bumping into him as McGuire hurried around the car and opened the back door of the sedan.

"Excuse me," said Vince as he grabbed the man by the arm while jamming his .38 pistol into his ribs. "Get in the car very quietly."

Mac Telford gave the stranger a questioning look, then looked down at the gun he held. "Just take my wallet and go," he said as he glanced around the street for help. He was a talented litigator, a quick thinker, but he had never been confronted with a gun in his gut.

"Get in the fuckin' car," said the man again with a growing anger.

"Fight, flee, or obey," were the words he remembered coming from a self-defense instructor a thousand years ago. "You've got just seconds to make that decision," the man had taught. "After that, the bad guy is in control."

Uncharacteristic indecision on Mac's part caused those precious seconds to tick away. Mac's only hope was that he could talk his way out of this mess. He looked the stranger in the eye and said again, "You've got the wrong man."

Vince violently pushed the man towards the sedan while yelling, "Get in the fuckin' car," as ten or fifteen shocked bystanders looked on.

***

Watching the morning news as he worked out, Jimmy White nearly fell off his elliptical trainer when the reporter said, "Police are asking for help to find a Midtown man who was apparently abducted in the area of East 33rd and Lexington Avenue last night about six pm. Mac Anthony Telford, a well-known Manhattan attorney, was walking home when two men forced him into a gray sedan. Telford's wife later reported him missing. If you have information, or saw anything in that area, please contact Crime Stoppers at the number on the screen."

Stepping off the trainer, Jimmy wiped the sweat off his face with a towel before picking up his phone and calling Frankie DiPiero.

White didn't observe the usual pleasantries. When Frankie answered, he said, "Did you grab the attorney?"

"What are you talkin' about?" asked DiPiero.

"Somebody grabbed Tinsley's attorney Telford last night," said Jimmy. "Was it you guys? It's all over the news."

Frankie felt his ulcer flare up as he recalled the conversation with his impulsive younger brother about the attorney. "I don't know anything about that," he answered truthfully.

"Did Vince get to him?" asked Jimmy. "This might be the bonehead move from which your family can't recover. This might be the tremor that causes your castle to crumble. I told you to control that son of a bitch."

"I don't know," said Frankie again. "I'll call Vince and get back to you."

Frankie hung up the phone then picked it up again to call his brother, then dropped the receiver back on the phone and decided to instead to drive the short distance over to his house.

Using his key to Vince's backdoor, Frankie let himself in. He found him in his bedroom, sound asleep, fully clothed, lying face down on top of the covers of his bed. Kicking the mattress as hard as he could without injuring his foot, he yelled, "What did you do?"

Vince rolled over with a start and blinked a few times. "Get out of my bedroom," he said angrily.

"What did you do with the attorney?" Frankie yelled.

"I asked him a few questions," said Vince with a chuckle. His headache from an evening of drinking too much scotch caused his smile to quickly fade. "Get out of here."

"It's all over the news; there's witnesses! This could take us down and land our asses in prison. This could take the entire family down," Frankie yelled. "What did you do to the attorney?"

Hangover or not, Vince had taken all the abuse from his brother he was going to take. Years of being told he was overly impulsive and not smart enough to run the family businesses welled up inside him. "I took care of it," he yelled back at his older brother as he sat up in bed. "I asked him where Tinsley was, and when he wouldn't tell me, I busted his knee. Then I busted the other one."

Frankie put his hand on his forehead and looked up to the ceiling. "Where the fuck is he right now?"

"We stuffed him into a fifty-five-gallon barrel and buried his body under that new warehouse you're building up in Hackensack. He'll be under a concrete floor in a few days."

Frankie thought he might throw up. "Oh no, Vinnie," he said in a quiet voice. "There were witnesses on the street. They can finger you. The investigation could take down everything the old man built. You may have really screwed up this time."

"Nobody's going to finger me, and nobody's going to find the body. No body, no crime, right?" said Vince with a smile.

As Frankie sat down on the edge of his brother's bed with his face in his hands. An excavation contractor that he had hired was digging a utility trench across a Hackensack lot that had been staked out for a new warehouse. Ten minutes into the dig, his backhoe brought up a yellow fifty-five-gallon barrel.

***

Jodi couldn't relax as she made her way to the office. Everybody looked suspicious and everybody seemed to be watching her. "You're just being paranoid," she told herself over and over. When she spotted the front door of her office building, a place she felt relatively safe, she resisted the urge to run, but she walked as fast as she could.

After hanging up her coat and booting up her computer, she walked into the breakroom for a cup of coffee. The TV mounted in the corner of the room was almost always on. As she mixed cream into her coffee, the local news replayed the story of the abducted attorney. Hearing Mac's name, Jodi quickly wheeled around, spilling her coffee. Half of the TV screen was filled with a picture of a much younger Mac Telford.

Melissa knew something was amiss the moment she walked into the breakroom. Jodi's hands covered her mouth as she stood next to a puddle of spilled coffee. She stared at the TV, which was now reporting on the day's weather. "What's going on?" she asked her friend.

"They got him," Jodi said as she pointed to the Channel Four weatherman.

"They got who?" Melissa asked.

Jodi didn't answer; she rushed out of the room, leaving her coffee cup sitting in the spilled coffee on the counter. Her mind was spinning. If the DiPiero family would abduct Mac on a busy street in an attempt to find Charles, they wouldn't let the fact that she was a woman stop them from getting to her.

She had to get out of town, she had to run, she had to hide. She had to get to Charles, wherever he was. Charles would know how to hide the two of them and how to protect them. She had to get to him, but she didn't even know which direction to go. She went to her desk and retrieved the phone number he had given her from her purse. Sitting at her desk, she fumbled through the phonebook until she found the section that decoded the area codes. The phone number was a Louisiana area code.

Grabbing her coat and purse, she started towards the door, when Melissa returned from cleaning up her coffee. "Jodi, what the hell is going on?" she said demandingly.

Jodi looked at her friend with wild eyes, then looked around at all the faces in the office that were staring at her. Her simple presence might be endangering her co-workers as she imagined a large Italian man bursting through the door with a gun and opening fire.

"I can't stay here. I have to go," she said.

Melissa grabbed her arm as Jodi started towards the door. "Stop! Tell me what's going on!"

Hearing the chaos erupting outside his office, Eric Miller walked out to a confusing scene. Melissa and Jodi were engaged in some sort of a tug of war. Melissa kept repeating "Tell me what's going on" while refusing to release Jodi's arm. The other secretaries and paras looked on in shocked amazement.

"Hey!" he said loudly. "What is going on?" Both women stopped struggling and looked at him. Melissa's face showed concern, but he hardly recognized Jodi through the look of fear and distress that distorted her face. "Let her go," Mills said to Melissa. The moment she did, Jodi bolted for the door. She didn't hear them yelling at her to stop.

Joe Quintero was enjoying an order of scrambled eggs and hash browns, when out of the corner of his eye, he spotted Jodi bolting from the front door across the street. She was moving fast. She looked white, frightened, as if she had just seen a ghost. By the time he finished chewing, left a ten-dollar bill on the table, and got to the door, she was gone. He headed for her normal bus stop but didn't find her there.

"Something's happened," Quintero reported to Jimmy White over the phone. "She's running. I'll head for her house to see if I can find her,"

"Damn," said White. "She must have just heard about the attorney."

"The attorney? Telford?" Joe asked.

"Yeah, Vince got to him. The news is reporting that he was grabbed on the street yesterday by two thugs, forced into a car. They haven't seen him since."

"There's witnesses?" Quintero asked in amazement.

"Several," said White as he shook his head. "Call me back in thirty minutes," he told Quintero. "I've got another call coming in. Hello," White said, picking up his other phone.

"Mister Verhei? This is Eric Mills, from Jodi's office," said the voice. "I wanted to call you. We're not sure what to do. Jodi came into work like normal this morning, but something has happened. About twenty minutes ago, she left here in a panic. We couldn't stop her; she looked scared."

"Did she say anything?" asked White in his best "concerned uncle" voice.

"She just said something about them getting him then ran out the door. I've got some of my staff out looking for her and I'm going to drive over to her house to see if she's there. I wanted you to know. It wasn't like her at all."

"Thank you for letting me know, Mister Mills. I'll put aside our silly family quarrels and call her mother to let her know that Jodi may be suffering from some sort of grief-related panic attack. Please call me back if you learn anything else."

After hanging up, White called Frankie DiPiero. "The girl's running. We've lost her."

"Vince buried the attorney," admitted Frankie. "We need to talk about damage control."

White shook his head and looked at the floor. "Not this time, Frankie. I think Vince may have finally screwed the pooch. I won't go down with you and your stupid brother. I'm out."

Both fear and anger welled up inside Frankie DiPiero. People didn't quit his organization; Frankie made the decision when they were done. But at the same time, he feared that White was correct. Vince's actions were probably going to cause problems for a long time to come. He needed time to think. He hung up the phone without saying "goodbye," then looked at his brother dozing on the bed next to him. He slapped him in the side of the head for the first time since he was fifteen.

***

The payphone at Dean's Bakery was mounted on the back wall next to the single unisex bathroom. Jodi rushed in and started plugging quarters into the phone as she dug them from the bottom of her purse. As she punched in the number Charles had given her, a man on the sidewalk stopped and looked in the window. She quickly turned her back to him, and when she looked again, he was gone.

After five rings, the phone connected to a voicemail with a man's voice that simply said, "Leave a message."

"Charles," Jodi said into the phone, cupping the voice piece with her hand so nobody could hear. "They've kidnapped Mac. He's missing. I'm so scared, I don't know what to do. I've got to get out of town before they get me."

Not knowing what action to take next, knowing she couldn't wait by the payphone for him to call her back at the bakery, she hung up and headed out the back door.

***

A silvery frost had taken the place of the melted snow of the previous mornings. Charles stood on the porch of the bunkhouse with a cup of coffee, his coat zipped to fend off the cold. The freezing morning temperatures had accelerated the changing of the leaves on the trees below the ranch, quickly turning them from green to brilliant shades of gold and red. In the rising sun, they didn't even look real against the backdrop of the evergreens behind them.

"God, this place is beautiful," he said to himself before noticing Mark standing on the porch of the main house. His coat was buttoned up and his hand wrapped around a steaming cup of coffee. Mark gave a simple nod. Charles slightly raised his cup in a return gesture.

After a few minutes, Mark swallowed the last of his coffee, set his cup on the porch railing, and walked to the bunkhouse. "How's that south line coming along?" he asked as he approached.

"Finished it yesterday. I'm working along the western bottom now," said Charles. He took a humble pride in the surprised look on Mark's face.

"We're going to do something a little different today," said Mark. "Fella up near Hungry Horse has a bull I want to take a look at. I'm going to have you run up there with me. You like to fish?"

"I've never been fishing," Charles answered truthfully.

Mark looked at the ground and shook his head. "Good lord, it's a wonder I don't have to teach you how to piss." He looked up with a smile. "I'll toss in some gear. There's a great stream up that way, the water's low this time of year, and the brookies are big. If you don't mind the cool temperatures, even you might catch something today."

Charles smiled. He really wanted to finish up the fence line; it had become a project he was proud of, something he was mentally invested in. But if his boss wanted him to go fishing, how could he resist? He nodded at Mark.

"You go feed the horses. Check that lower stock tank to see if it froze over last night. Bust the ice up a little if it did. We'll leave in an hour or so," said Mark as he turned back towards the house.

After driving up to the funny little town of Hungry Horse, they looked at a bull owned by a stout little guy named Floyd. In town, they had a decent burger and a milkshake at the Willows, a little tourist place that sold huckleberry jam, pies, and t-shirts. Then they drove a few miles east to Royal Creek and parked off the gravel road near a small meadow.

As they sat on the tailgate of Mark's truck, he taught Charles some of the simple knots to use to tie on tippet and flies. Then, standing in the road, he showed him the casting motion and made him practice it until he had it down. While Charles was fumbling with knots or wrapping line around himself, Mark talked about the art and theories around fly fishing.

Charles was always amazed at Mark's patience as an instructor. Whether cutting brush, grading a bull, or flinging fake bugs through the air with a fly rod, Mark explained the moving parts and the background of each technique or piece of equipment. In forty minutes, Charles had become a reasonably proficient beginner fly fisherman, according to Mark. "Now it's time to go get really tangled up."

They walked across the meadow to the small creek, where Mark showed him how to read the water. He showed him which rocks likely had small trout lying near them. Then he demonstrated how to land his fly on the water above the rock or log so it would float past, replicating a bug in the water. On his third cast, Mark caught a twelve-inch brook trout. After showing Charles how to land and unhook the fish without hurting it, he released it back into the stream.

"All this work and all this equipment and then you let the fish go?" asked Charles.

Mark smiled. "Yep, the thrill is in the hunt and the fight. We'll put him back, let him grow, and catch him again next summer when he's fourteen inches."

After a few hours of tangles, trips, falls, and hooks stuck in his fingers, Charles had caught a few small fish. Each had been a thrill. He was hooked on the sport.

***

The cabbie had dropped Jodi two blocks from her home. She slinked her way down the street and through a narrow passageway that led to the alley behind the brownstone. At the backdoor, she peered inside, looking for any movement, listening to see if anybody was moving around her home. She quietly opened the door and stepped inside, ready to bolt out at a moment's notice if she detected anyone in the house. After searching each room, she finally convinced herself she was alone.

Just as she was beginning to calm, the doorbell rang. She hid in her bedroom while somebody persistently rang the doorbell and knocked at the front door. From her bedroom window, she was able to look down on the street and see Eric's car. She ignored him, even as he knocked at the back door and yelled her name. He finally gave up and left.

Jodi spent all of the morning trying to figure out what to do. By early afternoon, her mind was made up; she had to get out while she could. After packing two bags, just the essentials, she tucked some important documents, including her passport and their marriage license, into a third.

She took one last look around their home, making sure she wasn't leaving behind anything important. She remembered her father saying, "I've never seen a hearse pulling a U-Haul trailer. You can't take it with you." The only thing she added were two framed pictures of the two of them. Nothing else mattered.

She made her way down the same alley that Charles had used for his last escape, not knowing she was experiencing the same fears he had been that morning, expecting someone to jump out of the shadows at any moment. Once she made it to the old Volvo station wagon, she tossed the bags inside then prayed it would start. She hadn't driven it in over a month. The engine sluggishly cranked over several times and finally started with what sounded like the battery's last breath.

Driving south, she crossed the Verrazano-Narrows Bridge into Staten Island before exiting I-278. Pulling into a gas station, she filled the car's tank using her credit card. When the transaction was completed, she threw the credit card in the trash. At the Chase Bank branch across the street, she withdrew five thousand dollars in cash. At a payphone across the street, she called the number Charles had given her again. She got the same short message and left hers, simply saying, "I'm on the run, heading out of the city. I'll call you back tonight at ten eastern time."

Her mind was swimming with thoughts and worries. She looked around the parking lot to see if anyone was paying undue attention to her. Leaving the bank and driving back towards I-278, she spent as much time looking in her rearview mirror as she did out the windshield. She was petrified that the FBI or the mob might be following her.

Traffic out of the city was always bad, worse during the evening rush hour. She kept a vigilant watch on the cars behind her, but rather than noticing mobsters and G-men, she saw the skyline and wondered to herself if she would ever see it again.

In her rearview mirror, all she could see was the sun-painted shrinking skyline of the place she had called home. Traffic started to speed up; she was westbound with the hammer down. She had no idea what direction to drive. North didn't seem right; she couldn't imagine Charles going towards Canada. South or west were her best bets. Getting away from the city was her only goal at the moment.

***

Vince smiled when his "guy" called him saying that the Volvo was on the move. The geek he had hired used a software system that determined which cell towers a cell phone hidden beneath the dash was hitting. It didn't give them an exact location, only a fifteen- or twenty-mile circle. The Volvo, however, was moving south and west, now pinging cellular towers on Staten Island.

"Go get the car," he said to Huey. "We're going for a drive."

Frankie looked up from the stack of papers on his desk. "Where are we going?"

"Tinsley's wife is making a run for it in her Volvo. Let's go see if we can find her."

Frankie shook his head. The last thing he wanted to do was to go on a wild goose chase, but at the same time, he didn't want his brother out there running around unsupervised. If he didn't go, Vince would go after Jodi Tinsley by himself. If he found her, God knows what trouble he might create. The last thing they needed right now was more trouble. He got up and begrudgingly put on his jacket.

As Huey drove, Vince sat in the passenger's seat and directed him. Every fifteen minutes or so, Vince would receive a call from some guy named Matt who would give vague updates on the Volvo's location. They took the I-278 out to Staten Island and back into New Jersey, where they picked up the Jersey Turnpike and drove south. In the backseat, Frankie opened a map and tried to plot the puzzling locations the guy on the phone was feeding to Vince.

After a confusing hour of stopping, starting, and arguing while Vince belittled Huey for his inability to read his mind, a clear pattern started to emerge. The Volvo was heading southwest on I-95.

In his parents' basement in Newark, Matt LaShay was having the time of his life. Having never met the man on the other end of the phone, he was convinced that he was helping some secret faction of the government track down a spy or a drug kingpin. All he really knew was that a friend of a friend knew a guy who needed help tracking a car. Matt received two hundred bucks up front, and fifty dollars a week to monitor the car's movements.

His community college tech degree and his interest in hacking were finally paying off. The process was simple enough. Matt purchased a pre-paid cell phone and gave his buddy Doug, the son of a locksmith, fifty bucks to help him get into the car. It took less than three minutes to duct tape the phone up under the dash of the beige Volvo then hard wire the phone's charger into the fuse box. At home, he programed his computer to alert him if the phone's signal moved from one cell tower to another.

When the phone started moving, weeks after Matt had installed it, he called the number he had been given and told the guy with a Jersey voice and attitude that the car was changing location.

Matt was excited to be tracking the "suspect vehicle." After talking to the Jersey guy, he ran to his parents' car and pulled all the road maps out of the glovebox. On the wall beside his computer, he taped a New York/New Jersey map over his Kate Hudson poster. Using a sharpie, he tracked the haphazard route given to him by different cell towers that picked up the phone's signal. The first calls to his "contact" were difficult; the guy was angry at the changing information. But once the signals started to indicate a clear direction down I-95, his contact became more appreciative of his efforts.

After a fifteen-minute break for dinner and another can of Mountain Dew, Matt settled in for what could be an interesting evening in front of his computer.

CHAPTER SIXTEEN

They fished until sundown. Charles caught a few, about half as many fish as he saw Mark catch. Back at the truck, they broke down their rods and packed everything away. "Let's find a steak somewhere on the way home," said Mark. Charles thought that was a great idea. He was starving.

At the Bandit Saloon in Columbia Falls, they enjoyed a cold beer and a decent steak before heading back towards the ranch. As they drove south, Mark talked in greater detail about his plans to get the Big Sky Ranch back up and operating as it once had. "I'm going to need a lot of help. I can't afford to hire much of it out," he said while glancing over at Charles. "What are your plans once you get your wife out of New York?"

Charles hadn't thought that far. His sole focus was getting Jodi out of the city in the spring. He wanted to get her to Montana, a place where he felt isolated and safe. "You've taken a big chance letting me stay with you. Are you willing to take in another fugitive?"

Mark laughed. "One, two, or three of us. At some point, what's it matter?"

"What are you running from?" Charles asked, since his boss had broached the subject.

Mark stared out the windshield for a several seconds before replying, "Unfortunate decisions based on bad advice a long time ago."

"Is somebody looking for you?" asked Charles.

Mark laughed. "I think we're all content the way things are. As long as I stay hidden and quiet, they won't put too much effort into looking for me."

Charles was intrigued; he had wondered what stories Mark had to tell, what his mysterious past held. "Is it the law or the bad guys looking for you?"

"What's the difference?" he asked as he picked up his flip phone from the truck's console. Noticing he had some messages, he pressed a couple of buttons to retrieve them. "Uh, oh," he said after a moment with the phone to his ear. "Both of these messages are for you."

***

Jodi drove south down I-95, worried about her car's ability to get her to wherever it was she needed to go. The old Volvo had been her mother's car for years. When her mother bought a new car, the dealer had offered her next to nothing in trade, so she instead gave it to Jodi. Charles and Jodi drove it fairly regularly until he got his company BMW. After that, the car sat idle, used only occasionally. The tires needed to be replaced and the check engine light had been on for a couple of years, but Jodi liked having her own car and it certainly was coming in handy at the moment.

Once she was free of the city, she felt like she could begin to breathe again. She stopped near Jamesburg to fuel the car and get a quick bite to eat, but she was always on the watch for thugs or FBI agents. It made her wonder if she would always be looking over her shoulder. She hoped Charles had truly found a place that made him feel safe.

Jodi kept plodding south and west on I-95 through Philadelphia, Wilmington, and Baltimore. She kept a close watch on the time, not wanting to miss her 10pm call to Charles. He had to answer this time, she thought. Why would he give her a number that nobody answered? She needed to hear his voice. She needed his reassurance that everything would be okay.

Near Bethesda, she felt that she had driven enough. She was tired, and it was nearly time to place her call. She checked in to a Comfort Inn just off the Beltway then made the call from the payphone outside of Applebee's across the street.

"Answer the damn phone," she said out loud as it started to ring. She heard his voice just after the second ring.

"Jode?" he asked with a tone of urgency.

Her emotions got the best of her. She broke down in tears, unable to speak at the sound of his voice on the other end of the line.

"Jodi, are you okay?" he asked in a bit of a panic. "Jodi, talk to me. Are you all right?"

She composed herself. "They got Mac," she said as she sniffled. "I'm afraid they'll get me next. I had to get out of town. Where are you?"

"Are you somewhere safe?" he asked.

"I just checked in to a hotel near Bethesda," she answered.

"Did you use your credit card to check in?" he asked in a concerned voice.

"No, I have cash. I threw my credit card away."

He was impressed with her thinking. "What makes you think somebody got Mac?" he asked.

"It's on the news. They grabbed him on the street, right in Midtown. They threw him in a car. Nobody's seen him since. I'm so scared," she said through her tears.

In his calmest, most reassuring voice, he said, "It's going to be okay. If you wait there a few days, I'll come get you."

"No," she said. "I can't wait. Tell me where to go and I'll come to you."

"It's a long drive," he warned.

"I don't care, as long as we're together."

His geography wasn't the sharpest when recalling the big states out west, but he needed to get her closer to him. "Head for South Dakota. Call me tomorrow night."

"South Dakota?" she asked in sarcastic tone. "You couldn't hide out in Barbados or somewhere warm?"

"We'll go anywhere you want to go," he replied. "I just have to get you to me so I can protect you."

"I'm just kidding, Chas," she said while wiping her tears. "As long as we're together, I don't care if we live in the middle of Kansas," She paused for a moment then said, "We don't live in the middle of Kansas, do we?"

"No, babe," he said with a laugh. "This place is so beautiful, I can't wait for you to see it. Every morning, I'm shocked at the incredible beauty of the mountains and valley that surround me."

"I can't wait to see it with you," she said. "I love you."

***

The Jersey boys were just north of Washington DC. Huey complained that he was hungry and Frankie asked how far they were willing to chase this girl. As Vince was telling them both to shut up, Matt LaShay called. "She may have stopped in the Bethesda area. The signal hasn't changed towers in over thirty minutes."

"How far to Bethesda?" Vince asked over his shoulder.

Frankie looked at the map. "About twenty-five miles."

"I'll bet she stopped there for the night," Vince said.

"Good," said Huey. "Let's find her and get back to Jersey."

"No way," answered Vince. "She's running to her husband. We're going to follow her to him then slowly kill the thieving bastard."

In the backseat, Frankie's butt and back hurt from the five hours in the car. He hoped Tinsley was hiding somewhere in the DC area but knew this could be just the beginning of a long trek. Killing Tinsley slowly, he thought to himself, it wasn't his style, but the kid had $2.7 million dollars of family money. He reminded himself that the reason he was along on this quest was to recover the money and to make sure that whatever Vince did to Tinsley was done in a discreet manner.

Just off the interstate in Bethesda, they found a Waffle House and a gas station next to each other. They fueled the Lincoln then watched in amazement as Huey ate nearly everything on the menu. After hearing from Matt that the car hadn't moved, they drove around the area looking for a beige Volvo wagon with New York plates in the parking lot of several hotels. After an hour of searching, they gave up and checked in to a Howard Johnson.

Two miles away, at the Comfort Inn, Jodi spread her newly purchased U.S. map across the bed. In the morning, she would drive towards Columbus, Ohio, then Indianapolis, then finally into Indiana and Iowa, eventually making her way into South Dakota. It looked like a long, lonely drive. But Charles was somewhere out there waiting for her. She was excited to see him, to hold him. She hoped nobody else was as eager to see the two of them.

After plotting out a course for the following day, Jodi turned off the light. She laid her head on the thick hotel pillow and cried.

***

There was a lot of excitement on the morning conference call. District attorneys from both New York and New Jersey were on the line along with police from both sides of the river. Four separate people had positively identified Vince DiPiero as one of the two men who pushed the Midtown attorney Mac Telford into the sedan on East 33rd. The excavator had dug up Telford's body, stuffed inside a fifty-five-gallon barrel, on a construction site owned by the DiPiero family. A treasure trove of evidence against DiPiero had been found. It looked like they finally had him on a murder charge.

"In the next half hour, we should have all the search and arrest warrants that we need," said New York Assistant District Attorney Tess Buttram. "Jersey City and Hackensack police departments are coordinating their efforts to raid multiple homes and businesses at the same time. Let's get this guy before he knows what hit him."

As Jersey City cops broke down Vince's front door and simultaneously burst into his warehouse office, he cussed as his cell phone woke him in Bethesda. It was the kid, Matt. The Volvo was moving. The phone under the dash was pinging cell towers to the west of DC.

***

After waking, Jodi quickly packed then carried her bag down to the lobby. On her way out of the hotel, she grabbed a cup of coffee and a pre-packaged Danish from the breakfast bar. Before walking out, she stood at the door, searching the parking lot for anybody who looked suspicious. At her car, she paused. Dropping to her knees, she looked under the car for anything that looked unusual. Realizing that she had never looked under the car before, she had no idea what was supposed to be there and what was not. She didn't see anything labeled "bomb," so she got in, took a deep breath, and started the car.

Her route took her northwest on I-270 up to I-70. Just twenty miles out of Washington DC, the traffic lightened up. The fall colors were out, and the maples and elms showed off their golden and red leaves. Jodi tried to focus on the beauty surrounding her rather than the danger she sensed was following her. Nothing in her rear-view mirror was out of the ordinary. She memorized the cars and trucks behind her, as far back as she could see. They came and went, exiting here or there, falling back out of her sight or coming up from behind and passing her. None of them remained the same. She had no reason to think she was being followed. It was just something she could feel.

***

It took Vince a half hour to get Huey and Frankie up and in the car. Huey complained that he needed more sleep and Frankie wanted a shower and a decent breakfast before the day's wild goose chase began. By the time they finally got moving, it was clear that the Volvo was heading northwest. In the backseat, Frankie looked at the map and tried to make sense of her route. Driving southwest to the Washington area then turning to the northwest could only mean they were close to her final destination. Or she was trying to throw off anybody who might be tailing her. She might zigzag all the way across the country to Los Angeles or Seattle for all they knew.

Vince's cell phone rang, but he didn't recognize the number. "Yeah?"

"Vinnie, it's Linda," said his secretary in a stressed, whispery voice. "Where are you?"

"Down near D.C.," he said. "Where are you?"

"I'm at the payphone by the liquor store. The cops are in your office and the warehouse, about twenty of them with a search warrant. They are tossing everything. The guy that lives next to you called, saying they've raided your house too."

"Shit," replied Vince.

"What it is?" asked Frankie from the backseat.

"It's the cops," he said. "They just hit my house and the warehouse."

Frankie slapped the seat next to him. "That's just great. Your fucking brilliance is bringing down the entire family. We've got to get back to Jersey and see what we can save."

Vince turned around, his face was turning red. "No way. I'm not going to prison. We're going to find Tinsley and that $2.7 million. It's not much, but it's clean money. He stole it from us. They can't trace it. If we can get it back, we can start over somewhere else."

Laying his head back against the headrest and tightly shutting his eyes, Frankie tried to figure out what to do next. If the police and the Feds had raided Vinnie's house and office, there was no telling what information might find. Perhaps enough to obtain a warrant to search his office, perhaps enough to start unraveling the web of corporations and layers of companies that shielded the family from the real sources of income.

If they were smart enough to figure it out, they would find enough evidence to convict him of a hundred different crimes from drugs to tax evasion. It was all there, cleverly disguised, and not impossible to decipher. He could imagine it all falling apart, a hundred-million-dollar empire crumbling to the ground, all because of his impulsive little brother. A hundred million dollars at stake and they were chasing some young woman, hoping to find $2.7 million dollars.

Vince's phone rang again with another update on the Volvo's location. Frankie was suddenly struck with the irony of Vince's cell phone. "Vinnie! Your phone; the cops are probably tracking us right now!"

Vince ended the call with Matt and looked at the phone for a second. "No way," he said. "It's not my phone. I had my girlfriend's stepdaughter sign the contract for me. Everything's in her name. They can't tie it back to me."

In the backseat, Frankie closed his eyes again and hoped Vince was telling the truth. He hoped his little brother had done something right, just this once.

***

Charles felt helpless. There was nothing he could do until Jodi called him again. His wife was alone and vulnerable, perhaps being pursued by the DiPiero brothers, maybe even the Feds, and all he could do was wait for her call.

Mark knew Charles was incredibly distracted. Asking him to ride fence line wasn't fair. Besides, in his current state, he would probably nail his hand to a fence post. The weather report showed another front coming in from the northwest the day after next. It would bring a chance of snow to the valley. Mark figured it was a good day to stay close to Charles, so together, they would work on buttoning up the barn and winterizing some of the equipment around the ranch.

They spent the morning in the barn fixing the tracks on the hayloft doors so the doors could be closed for the first time since Mark had owned the ranch. When they were done, the large doors rolled open and closed easily. Several times, Mark caught Charles looking down towards the front gate, as if he was hoping to see her car appear. He could feel his anxiety and his impatient excitement, but the only thing he could do to help the poor guy was to keep him busy.

At lunchtime, they went up to the main house, where Mark heated up some chili he had made a few nights earlier. After eating, he suggested they do some shooting. Charles seemed more excited to shoot holes in things than to winterize the old tractor, and Mark was okay with that given the circumstances.

Just above the ranch house, up against a hillside, Mark had found an area that had long ago been used as a dump of sorts. The ground was scattered with old rusty tin cans and bottles that had likely been there since the forties or fifties. He had always intended to clean up the area. His way of doing that was to use the cans for targets, picking up a bag of tin and glass each time he was up there.

They set up about twenty cans in various locations against the hillside and moved back nearly fifty yards to Mark's truck. Mark pulled out a variety of weapons: a 30.06 with a scope, an AK-47 he had picked up in a horse trade, the old 30-30 saddle gun, and a few others. He laid them on a blanket in the bed of the truck and explained the differences in each to Charles before instructing him on how to load and fire each.

Mark couldn't get over the young man's steady hand and good eyesight. His ability to hit even small targets at a distance was uncanny. He wished his vision was still that sharp, but even before age had stolen his decent eyesight, he knew he had never been that steady of a shooter.

***

A dark mood filled the Lincoln as Vince pushed Huey to drive faster while Frankie warned him against getting pulled over. All three of them were likely fugitives by now. With only one cell phone among them, Vince tried to keep updated on Jodi's route while Frankie was trying to get meaningful information from home.

A steady stream of calls was coming from Kelly McGuire, various business partners, family, and even Jimmy White. They all told the same story: the police had raided and were now carrying boxes of papers, computers, and numerous other items out of homes, offices, and warehouses owned by DiPiero family members. It was all coming apart as the two boys, left in charge of their father's dynasty, were rocketing towards Ohio, chasing a young woman who might be running towards the man who had started their downfall.

As more information came to them, Frankie decided that being out of New Jersey was probably a good move. They were one step ahead of the law, they weren't under arrest, and they were putting miles between them and various associates who might soon be arrested and charged with crimes for being associated with the family. Jimmy White had made it clear that if his name was attached to any of their crimes, the brothers wouldn't have to worry about prison. They wouldn't live that long. Frankie warned Vince not to tell anybody, even their closest allies and relatives, where they were.

Calls started coming in from family members whose properties were being raided and searched. By noon, police searches had extended to cousins and friends who had absolutely no business connections to the brothers. "It's a blood bath," said Frankie as he tossed the cell phone into the front seat and covered his eyes. "They just served Momma with a search warrant."

Vince blew up, shouting a tirade of curse words and threats while punching the ceiling of the car. Baby Huey kept quiet and pushed west as fast as he could without getting pulled over. He had never wanted out of a car so bad in his entire life.

***

Jodi kept pushing, praying every mile that her car would keep running as she made her way through Ohio and into Indiana. She thought central Illinois would be a good stopping point for the night while battling fatigue and the aches and pains caused by a very old and very well-used driver's seat. She promised herself she would only eat and pee when she was forced to stop for gas, and she tried her best to hold to that schedule. The peanut-sized baby in her womb seemed to be sitting right on the top of her bladder. She couldn't believe that something so small could cause her to need to urinate so badly.

As she drove, she stayed vigilant to the cars around her, always watching for one that stayed in her sight for too long. At gas stations and rest areas, she scrutinized anybody who looked her way. She tried to tell herself again and again that she was just being paranoid, but she couldn't shake the feeling that she was being followed. She tried to relax and get herself to enjoy the amazing scenery, but she knew she wasn't on vacation. Her vigilance might save her life, and it might save Charles' life too.

"Push through the fatigue, push through the pain of a really bad seat, push past the fear," she told herself. Charles was somewhere out there, and if she could keep going, if her car would keep running, she would eventually get to him.

***

Charles paced back and forth in the bunkhouse as he watched the clock move toward 8pm at a painfully slow tempo. He didn't know what he would do if she didn't call. He held Mark's fully charged cell phone in his hand and prayed for it to ring. At two minutes before the hour, he started to feel panic setting in, thinking of all of the things that might have happened during her day that could prevent her from calling. The most alarming thought was that the DiPiero boys had caught up with her. The most terrifying, however, was that she had changed her mind and decided to go back home and find a man who wasn't so difficult to love.

As his fears and insecurities begin to overwhelm him in the silence of the bunkhouse, the phone in his hand started to ring. "Jode?" he answered quickly.

"Hi, Chas," she said in an upbeat tone. "I made it to Champaign, Illinois. God, this is one big country," she quipped.

"Is everything okay?" he asked.

"Other than being tired from a lot of driving, everything's great. Will I see you tomorrow?" she asked.

He looked at the map spread on the table and found Champaign. His heart sank when he saw the distance she still had to cover. "No," he said with a sigh. "I'm in Montana. If you think it's a long way from New York to Champaign, Illinois, wait until you get to South Dakota. You've never seen so much empty space in your entire life."

"Montana?" Jodi said with a hint of laughter. "Why did you pick Montana? I hear that Upstate New York has some out-of-the-way places, and it's a hell of a lot closer to Brooklyn."

Charles felt guilty for making her drive so far. "I don't know, babe. This place sort of picked me," he admitted. He got down to business and tried to find the best route for her to get north, where she could pick up I-90. If she was to take I-74 north, it became I-80 as it crossed into Iowa. At Iowa City, she could take I-380 north through Cedar Rapids, Waterloo, Fort Dodge, and finally north to I-90 in southern Minnesota.

The names of the towns sounded like mythical places from the long-forgotten storybooks of her youth. Jodi was disheartened that she would have to spend another night somewhere out in South Dakota alone, but she was happy to hear that there was a light at the end of the tunnel. Montana was a state she knew nothing about. In her mind, it conjured up thoughts of cowboys and Indians, and it seemed like it would be a cold place with tall mountains. Other than those images, put there by books or movies from her past, she had no idea what to expect.

She didn't want to let him off the phone. His voice was all she had to hold on to at that moment. She made him tell her about the ranch and the valley. She laughed when he told her he wore jeans every day. There was a difference in his voice, something new, something calm, and something that projected an excitement about his new life.

When she finally admitted that she was too cold and too tired to continue standing at the truck stop payphone, they professed their love for each other one last time before she drove a few blocks down the route to her hotel room at the Ramada. She crawled into bed with a warm smile on her face and dreamt about being held by her husband once again.

CHAPTER SEVENTEEN

The Jersey boys were physically and emotionally spent as they pulled into the Red Roof Inn just off the interstate near Champaign. Matt LaShay had called, saying the Volvo's signal had quit moving. She was likely there for the night. The timing matched up with her approximate stopping time in Bethesda the night before. They didn't take time to look for her car. They were all too tired after an incredibly emotional day.

Frankie went to his room and collapsed on his bed. His father's empire, the family business that had been entrusted to him, was crumbling as they chased a young lady across the country. They lived on a hope that she would lead them to her husband and a relatively small amount of stolen money.

At least they were doing something. Frankie knew that If he returned home, he and Vince would likely be arrested and eventually prosecuted for numerous crimes, including murder. Depending on what the cops had found in the search of their homes and offices, he too would face charges. He was a man who had been wearing the same clothes for two days, a man without a home, a man without a future.

He closed his eyes and tried to figure out what his father would do. He kept coming back to the obvious. His father would have kept Vince and the stockbroker under control. Frankie had failed him, he had ruined the family, and he had ruined everything his father had built. He fell asleep on top of the covers as the faces of his mother, his cousins, his aunts and uncles, his nieces and nephews, all the people the family supported looked to him for a solution.

***

With his cup of coffee in hand and his coat collar pulled up, Mark walked out onto the porch of the main house before the rising sun lit the tops of the western range. He was startled when Charles yelled over from the bunkhouse that breakfast was on. He waved and walked through an inch of freshly fallen snow, kicking the white powder off his boots before entering the little building.

"What's all this?" he asked his hand as he looked at a huge breakfast laid out on the table. Charles was at the stove cooking more. "Are you expecting the Seventh Army to show up?"

"I just felt like making a big breakfast this morning," said Charles in a spry tone. "I hope you brought your appetite."

"Did you talk with your wife last night?" Mark asked.

"Yeah," he answered as he spun around. "She made it to Champaign, Illinois. She should be able to get to Sioux Falls or beyond today. That would put her here tomorrow night!"

"That's great news," replied Mark. No wonder the guy was in such great spirits.

As they ate breakfast, they talked about fixing up the bunkhouse a bit for her arrival. "Let's run into town and buy some curtains for the windows," said Mark. "Maybe we should get a tablecloth and an arrangement of those plastic flowers for the table. Let's dress the place up a little. Sorry about the bunk beds; they're attached to the walls. I can't do much to make the sleeping arrangements better right away."

Charles looked at the single bunks. "I don't think we'll be sleeping very far apart for a few days," he said with a grin. "We'll work out something after that."

***

"Get your butts out of bed," yelled Frankie as he banged on the side-by-side doors of Huey and Vince. "Let's get going,"

Vince opened his door. His hair was disheveled and his eyes were barely open as he stood in his doorway in his white t-shirt and underwear. "I haven't heard from my guy yet. Where are we going?"

"We're two hours south of Chicago," said a very awake Frankie. "That's where he dumped the BMW, so that's where I figure she's going. Let's get ahead of her. We'll stop somewhere north and wait for her. I want this asshole in the bag before lunch."

Vince liked his older brother's reasoning, which was a rare occurrence. "Wake up the kid," he said while pointing next door. "I'll be ready to go in ten minutes."

It took them forty-five minutes to get Huey up, get the car fueled, and get on the road. Vince called Matt LaShay, but the kid didn't answer. They drove north towards Chicago on Frankie's gut instinct. Vince tried to call Kelly McGuire and a few others to find out the latest on their problems piling up in New Jersey, but nobody was answering their phones. It became silent inside the Lincoln. Nobody talked, and they kept to themselves, each wondering their own fate.

***

Jodi couldn't believe she had slept so late. It was daylight, nearly eight in the morning when she got out of bed. She hurried to get ready then sprinted to her car, more worried about gobbling up the miles between them than about mobsters or car bombs. As she filled her tank at the same gas station the DiPiero brothers had used a half an hour earlier, she reminded herself that she needed to remain vigilant.

She flew up I-74 trying to make up time, making it to Bloomington in a blistering thirty-five minutes. She slowed down after seeing a state policeman with another car pulled over. She didn't need a ticket or a public record showing where she had been.

***

The DiPieros had made it to Oak Lawn, Illinois, just south of Chicago, when the phone rang. Vince answered it, then went into a tirade, cussing at the person on the other end before tossing the phone onto the car's dash. He reached into the backseat and ripped the map from Frankie's hands. "Your stupid hunch just cost us a bunch of time. She's damn near to Iowa!"

"Well, your stupid-ass kid didn't give us any updates until now. We could have sat in our rooms or we could have gone with my hunch." Frankie was tired of Vince's constant belittling, and he was tired of sitting in the back of the car. He was tired of the inconsistent and vague updates from some kid. He wanted everything to be normal again, but it didn't seem like things would ever be a normal again. He was frustrated, tired, scared, and perfectly fine with taking it all out on his little brother.

***

I-74 turned north at Galesburg and forty miles after that intersected with I-80. Jodi was making great time, and the feeling that she was being followed faded. She relaxed and began to enjoy her journey. At a gas station near Iowa City, while her gas tank filled, she spread her map on the hood of her car. An older, kind-looking gentleman wearing overalls noticed her map and introduced himself as Lester before asking where she was going.

"Sioux Falls," she replied to the kind-looking man. "I was thinking about turning north here, driving through Waterloo, and picking up I-90 in Austin."

The man looked at the map. "That will get you there, and it's a pretty drive with a lot of small towns. But if you're in a hurry, stay on 80 through Des Moines, then follow the signs to Sioux Falls up I-29."

She thanked him, then he asked her if she wanted any apples. "Apples?" she asked.

"Yeah, me and my wife just picked up a bunch of apples from a friend up in Belle Plaine. They're pretty good. I'll go get you a couple."

She tried to turn him down, but he wasn't listening. He rushed to his car and returned with a sack containing about a dozen apples. She thanked him with a hug.

Pulling back onto I-80 with a smile on her face and a half-eaten apple in her hand, she felt that familiar feeling return. She looked in her rearview mirror and looked for suspicious cars but didn't see anything unusual. She pressed forward, pushing beyond the speed limit to put miles between her and some real or imagined threat behind her.

***

Vince had taken over tracking the girl's location on the map. It seemed from the updates that she was probably eighty to a hundred miles ahead of them, driving east towards Des Moines, Iowa. The mood in the car was dark. Vince spoke, but nobody responded to him. Frankie sat in the back seat, planning his next verbal jabs to his brother. Huey drove, thinking how much he hated this trip and how he was beginning to dislike the two men he idolized the most.

Huey wanted to go home. He was tired of driving and tired of his uncles' fighting. But he knew better than to say a word. He was hungry and his butt hurt, however, complaining would only send Frankie into another tirade. He knew they had to stop soon for fuel. He hoped they would take the time to eat a decent meal.

The day became a blur. Frankie kept speculating on where she was heading as he calculated the declining distance between them based on the vague reports he received from Matt. "I'll bet she's going to Omaha," he would say. When she turned north, he would pick some random location to the north and say, "Fargo, that's where she's going. I knew it."

They kept driving and the distance between them kept tightening. The only thing they could agree on was that South Dakota was the biggest, emptiest place they had ever seen. Huey had heard that everybody in the country hated city slickers. Vince silently worried about finding Tinsley hanging out with a bunch of armed cowboys. In the backseat, Frank worried about his crumbling empire and their mounting legal problems. He blamed everything on Vince and Charles Tinsley.

It was nearly 10pm when Vince's phone rang. All three of them gave a sigh of relief when Matt told him the Volvo had stopped moving somewhere near Rapid City, South Dakota, just twenty-five miles west of them. "We've got to buy some clothes tomorrow," said Frankie. "You guys stink," he said with a chuckle.

Just off the exit, they decided on a Best Western Hotel, which was close to both the Outback Steakhouse and Denny's restaurants. Frankie and Huey stood next to the car while Vince went in to see if they had three rooms. While the two stood in the cool night air, Huey entertained himself by looking at the different states' license plates in the parking lot. "Hey look, Uncle Frankie. There's one from New York."

Frankie turned to see him pointing at a beige Volvo station wagon with New York plates. "Well, son of a bitch," he said out loud. "Huey, pull the car around back and wait for us there."

Vince was walking across the lobby towards the front door with three keys and a smile as Frankie entered the hotel.

Vince quietly said to him, "There's a Volvo wagon in the parking lot with New York plates."

"You're fuckin kiddin' me," replied Vince. They talked briefly about what to do but ultimately decided to do nothing. The goal was to follow the girl to Tinsley. They would get some sleep, then Frankie would get up early to see if he could actually spot her. They didn't know for certain who was driving the Volvo, only assuming all this time that it was Tinsley's wife. They didn't want to tip her off that they were on her tail. The two brothers checked to see where Huey had parked. They didn't need her to spot a big Lincoln with New York tags. The kid had done well. There was no reason for her to drive around the backside of the hotel in the morning. Once they felt they had a plan in place, the three of them walked across the street for dinner before getting some sleep.

***

Charles was excited to hear her voice but even more excited to hear that she was so close to Montana. Barring any mechanical issues, she could be at the ranch in time for dinner the following day. As they spoke, he looked around the bunkhouse at the surprise he and Mark had prepared for her. Spending just over a hundred dollars at Kmart, they had transformed the old, barren bunkhouse into something that felt homey and comfortable. A framed painting of a field of tulips hung over the old unused stove pipe hole on the side of the wall. The table sported a new tablecloth and a bouquet of flowers. The bathroom was freshened up with new towels and a bright shower curtain. A patterned rug covered the area near the woodstove, where they arranged two rocking chairs with a small table between them.

"I can't wait for you to get here," Charles said.

Jodi was excited to see him as well but so tired from her twelve-hour drive. "I feel like I'm being followed," she told him. "But I don't know why. I haven't seen a suspicious car or person since I left Brooklyn. It's just a feeling."

"Just get here," he said. "Once you're here, everything will be fine. This place is safe, and it's so beautiful. Just think, tomorrow we'll be able to sleep in the same bed again. I'll keep you warm and secure."

It was exactly what Jodi needed to hear. She couldn't wait.

After a short night of sound sleep, her alarm went off at 5am. She showered, dried and curled her hair, then put on makeup. She was packed and downstairs in the lobby just as the staff was setting up the little breakfast bar. A few other people were in the little room off the lobby, an elderly couple, a young father with two small children whose wife was probably still sleeping, and a man in the corner engrossed in his newspaper. She selected a container of yogurt and some granola, then poured herself a cup of coffee and sat alone at a table facing the TV.

Frankie had never laid eyes on Jodi Tinsley until the moment she walked into the hotel's breakfast room. He recognized her immediately from her photo and was immediately taken by her beauty. He had seen many other women were more beautiful, but rarely had he seen somebody who was more naturally stunning. She was the type of woman who could pull her hair back in a pony tail and remove her makeup, and still turn heads. She was dressed in a sweater and slacks that accentuated every one of her perfect curves. Frankie found himself captivated by Tinsley's wife.

He continued to read his newspaper and sip on his coffee while carefully stealing casual glances at her. She ate quickly, refilled her coffee, and headed for the door. Frankie stood and walked to the lobby door, where he watched her climb into the Volvo and leave, then he turned quickly to wake up his cohorts. It was obvious to him, the way she was dressed, with her hair and makeup done, that today was the day she was reuniting with her husband.

Huey was getting used to these fire drill mornings. He was up and out the door in minutes after Frankie started pounding. He went to the car, started it to defrost the windshield, and fell asleep again waiting for his two uncles. He was awoken by the two of them as they crawled into the car. Both were excited by the prospect of finding Tinsley. Huey was just excited to end this cross-country circus. But based on the conversations he overheard, he wasn't sure what he might be returning to if he was to go back to Jersey. According to the reports Vince was getting by phone, several family members had been arrested for crimes ranging from drug trafficking to extortion to murder. Huey hadn't done any of those things, but he had been an accomplice and a witness to many things in his short life.

They rocketed east on I-90 towards Wyoming, pushing as hard as they dared in the growing daylight. They were forced to stop in Gillette for fuel, and Vince allowed them time to get breakfast at McDonalds before they got back on the road. Just short of Buffalo, Huey took his foot off the gas pedal, saying, "Is that her?"

A few hundred yards ahead of them on the interstate, he had spotted the beige Volvo with New York plates. In the often-hypnotic state of freeway travel, it would have been easy to drive right past her without noticing. Vince was impressed with the young man, but he would never say so.

"Back off and pull in behind this truck," said Vince while pointing to the big rig they were passing. They slowed down and followed her at a distance of almost a mile. The long, flat, and straight stretches of freeway with limited traffic made it easy to track the car at a great distance.

At Sheridan, Wyoming, she pulled off the freeway and into a truck stop for fuel. They were able to get gas at a station just across the road, hidden from her sight behind a U-Haul truck. While Huey filled the tank, Frankie ran inside the convenience store and loaded up on junk food and drinks. He spotted a pair of cheap binoculars and bought them as well.

***

"I'll go crazy if I don't do something today," Charles said to Mark over coffee. "The waiting will kill me."

Mark looked at his hand thoughtfully. "Okay, there's a cold front coming in—we might even get some snow—so I'll have you work inside. Finish up the hayloft up in the barn. I want all that plywood we laid screwed down securely. When you're done with that, figure out how to make that old hay trolley work again. You might keep the 30-30 nearby. You never know who might show up with your wife today."

A cold chill ran down his spine as Charles thought about the possibility of the Lincoln Continental New Jersey boys chasing Jodi. As he walked down to the barn, the old Winchester in his right hand, he thought about her running across the country with them in pursuit. He knew they were after him, that they wouldn't make their move until she led them to him. A strange comfort came over him in knowing they might be out there following her. They wouldn't let anything bad happen to her until she made it to him.

He climbed into the hayloft and slid the big doors open a few feet. He had an excellent view of the road that approached the ranch and the front gate. He would be able to see her coming for over a mile before she made the left hand turn through the gate onto the Big Sky. He leaned the gun up against the right door and went to work. The floor was huge. Charles figured he should put a screw in every foot. Each four by eight sheet would require twenty screws, and they had laid sixty sheets of plywood. Using a power screwdriver, he sank the first of twelve hundred screws into the new decking.

***

Jodi did a little happy dance in her seat as she crossed the Montana State line just north of Sheridan. Her celebration was cut short when it started snowing lightly about fifty miles outside of Billings. The snow wasn't sticking to the road, but the sight of it caused her stress. Growing up in New York, she had seen lots of snow, but she had never driven in it. When it snowed, she rode the bus or didn't go anywhere at all. Now she was miles from nowhere, in a hurry with bald tires, and no experience with winter driving. She prayed that it was just a dusting from a tiny storm and that the sun would reappear soon.

She turned on the radio and spun the dial until she found a station playing something other than country music. A few minutes later, the news and weather guy talked about a storm front approaching from the north. Her heart sank when he said Billings might receive up to six inches of snow. She pushed her foot down a little harder on the pedal. She was going to get in as many miles as she could while the getting was good.

A half mile behind her, Vince cussed as he saw the first snow began to fall. In the backseat, Frankie frantically scribbled notes of his conversations with the few friends, family, and business associates that would take his calls. Every call was worse than the last. The police seemed to be quickly finding their way through the spider web of companies, corporations, LLCs, and side interests that Frankie had set up to protect them from this type of attack. Authorities continued to raid properties, arrest associates, and dismantle everything he and his father had built.

The snow didn't last long, but the skies still looked ominous to the north. Jodi kept pushing, not knowing the boys were keeping her in sight. She stopped in Livingston to fuel up and used the restroom. After grabbing a quick bite to eat, she casually walked back to her car, but just as she reached for the door, the feeling in the back of her mind hit her again. They might not be far behind her. She looked around the parking lot for anybody suspicious then quickly got into her car and made her way back to the interstate.

Once Jodi pulled away, they were able to rush into the gas station and quickly fuel while Frankie bought more junk food in the convenience store. With a full tank, they sped down the freeway, chasing her while munching on old hotdogs and bags of corn chips.

Matt LaShay continued to track her, but the boys caught up to her again just before Whitehall. At Deer Park, she stopped for gas, a restroom, and food. Huey dropped Frankie at McDonalds to get some "real" food while Vince watched her from a vantage point across the street. Huey drove into town to gas up at a different station.

After fueling at the downtown Exxon, Huey returned to McDonalds to pick up his uncles. After climbing in the front passenger seat, Frankie said, "God, this car stinks. When we're done here, we're going to sell this thing and fly back to Jersey."

"I'm not sure we're ever going back to Jersey," said Frankie as he handed food to the two in the front seat. "How do you feel about wearing tropical shirts in the Caribbean?" Nobody answered him.

While the men choked down fast food in the Lincoln, Jodi enjoyed a decent salad at the truck stop café. She was deep in concentration, poring over her Montana state map, when the waitress brought her bill. "Where are you going?" she asked.

"Kalispell," answered Jodi. "It looks like I'll turn north on 93 just after Missoula."

"You'll save at least a half hour if you take the Avon exit just up the road, then follow the signs from there."

"And I won't get lost or eaten by bears going that way?" she asked the waitress with a smile.

The woman laughed. "Nah, the bears aren't a problem. You got to watch out for the men up that way. I grew up near Salmon Prairie. If you run into any problems up there, you tell them that you know Big Dara. I'm related to most of the folks up there. They'll take good care of you or I'll kick their butts."

Jodi smiled. "Thank you, Dara. I'm sure I'll be fine, but if I get lost or have car problems, I'll use your name."

Every time the girl had left the freeway over the last several days, the guys hoped that maybe that was her destination. When she took the exit to Avon and started driving north on a two-lane road, they really got excited. Getting off the freeway meant they were getting close to Tinsley. It was almost two in the afternoon. With any luck, their business would be done before dinner time and they would be celebrating with a couple of big steaks.

Following her on a lightly traveled two-lane road was much more difficult than on the busy freeway. They had to increase their distance from her to keep from being spotted and hope they saw her if she turned onto a side road. Just past Avon, it started snowing again.

CHAPTER EIGHTEEN

Charles stood and stretched his aching back after driving the last screw. He should have met her somewhere, he thought as he watched the snow start falling. He remembered she had never driven in the snow. He felt guilty that he hadn't at least replaced the bald tires on the old Volvo, but there had never been a need. It sat in the parking garage leaking oil and costing more than it was worth each year in registration and monthly parking fees, but they had kept it because it was a gift from Jodi's mother.

Charles pulled Mark's phone out of his coat pocket and looked. It showed no missed calls. He should have gotten her a cell phone, but she had never wanted one. They could have talked all day, he could have coached her through the snow, or he could have told her to stop at the next town and wait for him to come get her. He was anxious to hold her, knowing every minute she was getting closer, if the boys didn't catch up to her first.

Removing the ladder hanging on the wall, he placed it in the center of the loft and climbed it to take a look at the hay trolley, a contraption of rails, pulleys, and cables that brought hay up from the ground. Mark had asked him to fix it, however, before he arrived, he had never seen one. He was tasked with trying to figure out something he had never seen work. Charles smiled at the turn-of-the-century technology. It was a challenge he was going to enjoy.

***

Jodi focused so intently on the road ahead of her that she completely forgot about what might be following her.

Conditions rapidly deteriorated from bad to worse. Her knuckles turned white as she gripped the wheel harder, trying to will the car to stay on the road. The wipers on the old car were in predictably poor condition and soon the snow started to freeze on the windshield despite their efforts. She turned the defroster on high and was relieved when the ice began to clear. In just a matter of fifteen minutes, the road was completely covered. She followed the tracks of a car or truck that had passed this way before her, but she couldn't see anybody ahead of her through the falling snow. Glancing into her rearview mirror, she felt reassured that somebody was behind her. A set of headlights, perhaps a quarter mile back, calmed her nerves. She wasn't the only fool on the road.

Huey leaned forward, as if getting closer to the windshield would help him see better. They kept following the girl, hoping that she would reach Tinsley soon. The snow continued to fall and to accumulate on the road, making driving more difficult by the moment.

After a few hours of miserable driving, they reached the outskirts of Kalispell. Predictably, Vince said, "I'll bet this is it. This is where that son of a bitch is hiding."

Frankie glanced at the map on the seat next to him. "We're only about sixty miles south of the Canadian Border. For all we know, he might be a few thousand miles north, up in the Yukon Territory."

With that comment, Huey was done. "Fuck your money. I say we forget the money and forget the girl. I'm not driving you two into Canada. I'm going home."

Frankie leaned forward and lightly smacked the kid in the back of the head. "There might not be a home anymore; only a bunch of cops waiting to arrest you. Let's see what she does. We may need to rethink our plans."

"I'm not letting this bitch go," argued Vince. "Not after chasing her all the way across the damn country. We're going to get this guy and our money. If you want out, there's the door."

For a moment, Huey considered his offer. Opening the door and rolling out into the snow-covered street at thirty-five miles an hour sounded better than spending another five or six days tailing the Volvo, eating crap from convenience stores, and putting up with the constant abuse from his two loser uncles.

Nearing the middle of town, her right blinker came on. They followed her out Idaho Street with a renewed hope that the end of the chase was near. "Where's this road go?" asked Vince as they left town a few minutes later.

Frankie scoured his map. "Well, in about three miles, it turns south, back to where we came from. Or it turns north and heads up to some small towns in the mountains."

A few miles later, as the road turned south at the Lucky Pick Casino, she turned left onto Lake Blaine Road, continuing east towards the mountains. "We're close," said Vince with excitement. He reached under his coat to touch the grip of the .38 revolver he always carried in his shoulder holster. He knew it was there. It was just reassuring to feel it.

As Jodi turned at the casino, following the directions Charles had given her the night before, she felt the car slide. She panicked but remembered not to touch the brakes and allowed the car to recover from the slide. She remembered what her driver's education teacher had taught years ago. "Drive like there is a glass of wine on the hood of the car. Don't make any sharp turns or stops, and don't spill the wine."

She was so excited that she was so close to Charles. Headlights in her rearview mirror caught her attention. She looked, seeing a black sedan turning to follow her. She couldn't see the license plate. She didn't need to. She knew who it was. Spotting the Lincoln, her heart started sinking, thinking things were about to get worse. She pounded her fist against the steering wheel. She couldn't believe she had led the DiPiero brothers to Charles.

Her blood ran cold, and her mind raced. She didn't know what to do. Should she drive to Charles and hope she was able to warn him in time to protect himself? Could she could lead them away from him? Perhaps drive south towards Mexico and hope the hounds of hell nipping at her heels would follow. In her terror, she pushed the car as fast as she could without losing control, nearly missing the hard-right turn to the south.

"She's spotted us," said Huey as he noticed her driving become increasingly erratic.

"It don't matter; we're close," said Vince. "Maybe if we get our hands on her, Tinsley will come out of hiding and start throwing pens and staplers at us."

Jodi didn't know what to do. Her instincts told her to run to Charles. He always had the answers; he had always been her protector, her white knight. She needed him now more than ever. At Bench Drive, she turned left and nearly ended up in the ditch. The Lincoln had closed the distance between them despite her driving as fast as she could. The car followed her up the narrow side road.

A mile up Bench Drive, right where Charles said it would be, she spotted the large wooden sign that hung above the entrance to the Big Sky Ranch. She turned, but her front tires slipped across the slick road, out of control, and the front of her car slid into the ditch. She shifted into reverse and gunned the engine, but the car didn't move.

Charles was just finishing up his project in the waning light, when he heard a car's engine whine at high RPMs down near the road. He stepped to the opening in the loft's doors and gasped at the sight of Jodi's car in the ditch at the front gate. He was just about to run to her aid, when he spotted another car coming up the road, a black Lincoln.

Realizing she was stuck, Jodi looked over her shoulder to see the Lincoln stopping behind her. She struggled to get out of the car that was sitting at a strange angle. As she pushed the door, getting ready to run, a man flung it open, grabbed her by the arm, and yanked her from the Volvo.

Jodi struggled with him to get away. She swung and hit the face of a young, overweight man who held her with his left hand. He raised his right to hit her, but before he could deliver the blow, she heard a "whap." It sounded like a slab of bacon being dropped on the counter. The man released his grip and took a step backward as the sound of a shot rang out from the ranch above. Huey dropped to one knee while grasping his chest.

Before she could react, a second, older man grabbed her from behind by her coat collar and pulled her around the back of her car, ducking from the gunman somewhere up the hill from them. "Huey, are you okay?" asked Vince. Huey raised his hand slightly then fell forward onto all fours.

"Is Huey okay?" yelled Frankie from behind the Lincoln.

Vince peered around the corner of the car. Huey had fallen onto his back. "He's hit," said Vince.

"Where's the shooter?" asked Frankie.

"How the hell should I know," yelled Vince. He looked at the woman he held. "You steal our money then shoot my nephew? You two are going to wish you'd never been born when I'm done with you."

"We didn't steal any money," said Jodi. "Let me go, you prick."

"Your fancy pants husband took $2.7 million from my family. I'm going to get the money back, then I'm going to slowly cut the two of you into little pieces, and I'm going to enjoy every second of it."

Frankie yelled from behind the Lincoln, "Vinnie, we've got to get out of here. I'll get to the driver's seat and back around towards Huey, then you get the girl in the backseat."

"Don't move until we know where the shooter is," yelled Vince, but Frankie was already moving up the Lincoln's passenger side towards the car's front door. "Frankie, stop!" he yelled while he watched his brother climb into the right side of the car and struggle towards the driver's seat. He was trying to crawl over the console between the seats, when a shot hit him through the open driver's door.

"Fuck!" yelled Vince as his brother collapsed in the front of the car. Frankie never felt a thing. Judging by the bloody interior of the car, he had surely died instantly. Vince glanced around the corner of the Volvo. Huey wasn't moving. "Huey, are you okay?" he yelled but didn't get a response.

Vince put his revolver to Jodi's head and stood up slightly. "Tinsley!" he yelled. "I'll kill her, you know I will." He waited several seconds then yelled again. "I just want the money. I'll let her go and you'll never see me again if you just give me the money."

Lying prone on the floor of the barn, looking down the barrel of the saddle gun, Charles could barely make out what Vince was yelling. "What money?" he asked himself. He could see the top of a head through the window of the car, but he couldn't tell whose head it was. He didn't have a shot.

"Tinsley! Tell me you can hear me, or I'll kill her right now!" Vince yelled.

In the main house, Mark had been working on the books, when he heard the first shot. By the sound of the shot, he knew what gun had fired and what it meant. He heard a second shot from the Winchester as he pulled a rifle out of the gun cabinet. Jacking a shell in the chamber, he kneeled in the living room window, using the sill as a rest for his 30-06 Weatherby. Through the scope, he could see a body lying in the driveway and another slumped in the front seat of the black sedan.

He could see somebody hunched behind the station wagon in the ditch, but he didn't have a clear shot. Then a man leaned around the corner of the car and appeared to say something to the person lying in the drive before retreating behind the car again.

Mark Mulligan took a deep breath and said out loud, "Lord, give me one more good shot. That's all I ask." He aimed at the left rear corner of the wagon and waited.

Charles yelled out, "I can hear you. I don't have any of your money."

Jodi gasped at the distant sound of her husband's voice. She screamed as loud as she could, "Chas!!!"

Vince pushed her to the ground and pointed his .38 at her face. "Shut up. One more word and I swear I'll kill you right now." Holding her with one hand, he yelled out, "You've got $2.7 million from a stock sale the day before the attacks," Vince yelled.

"I don't have it," Charles yelled. "Let Jodi go, and when she's safe, I'll help you get it back," he shouted while recalling a transaction for about that amount. The funds were probably in his offshore sweep account. If Jodi was safe, he would happily give the guy his money. But Charles knew whichever DiPiero brother was hiding behind the Volvo with his wife wasn't leaving without the money and both of their heads.

Vince knew he couldn't let the girl go; she was the only thing between him and the sniper. He looked back at his dead brother in the Lincoln. His nephew was hit and lying on the ground. He was pinned down by a gunman who was in a better position with a better weapon. He didn't see a good outcome.

He decided to cut his losses, retreat to safety, and come back with more fire power than his snub-nosed .38. He would take the girl and make a run for it while firing towards the sniper to hopefully keep his head down. "Huey, get your ass off the ground. It's time to go," he yelled at his nephew. There was no response. "Huey! I need your gun."

Vince looked at his options. Going for the Lincoln was risky but using the girl as a human shield might work. If he could get the driver's door shut, then maybe he could get around to the passenger's side, pull Frankie out, then make the girl drive while he lay in the seat next to her. A few hundred yards down the road, he would be safely behind a stand of pine trees.

It was a horrible plan, Vince thought to himself. He had six shots in his little revolver and would be dragging the girl with him, using her for cover. But it was the only plan he could come up with, and he couldn't stay where he was.

Crouching, he leaned around the corner of the car, yelling, "Huey, you worthless son of a bitch, get your…" Jodi, lying on the ground behind, took advantage, and using both legs, kicked him in the butt as hard as she could. Vince lost his balance and tumbled out from behind the car. He struggled to get up, then she watched in horror as the top of his head exploded before he fell to the ground.

Jodi screamed in terror as she got up and started running. She ran in the direction of her husband's voice, her eyes wildly searching for Charles as she charged into the path of the gunfire.

The shot had surprised Charles, coming from somewhere behind the barn. He saw a man collapse next to Volvo before Jodi jumped up and started running in his direction. Charles didn't remember using the ladder from the loft to the barn floor. In seconds, he was on the ground and running out of the barn towards his wife.

Jodi ran away from the DiPiero brothers as fast as she could, screaming her husband's name. As she ran in the direction she had heard his voice, a bearded cowboy carrying a rifle came running out of the barn towards her. In her hysteria, she didn't know or care if the cowboy was a threat; she only knew that somewhere in the general direction she ran, she had heard her husband's voice.

The stranger ran towards her, yelling her name. It was his voice, but it wasn't Charles under the cowboy hat, behind the beard, or inside the coat and jeans. She tried to get around the cowboy, running towards the barn, screaming his name over and over. The cowboy grabbed her by the arm and pulled her to him, and she struggled until she saw his eyes and felt his familiar hug. He held her, telling her over and over that she was safe, everything was going to be okay.

Standing in the cold fading light of dusk in the lightly falling snow, they held each other. In his arms, hearing his voice, she felt a comfort she hadn't felt in a very long time.

A pickup truck bounced down the lane towards them. Charles didn't move, so Jodi didn't perceive the approaching vehicle as a threat. The truck stopped just a few yards from them. "I hate to break up your reunion, but we've got a mess to clean up before anybody drives by," said an older man from inside the cab.

Charles led Jodi to the passenger's side of Mark's truck and climbed in, still clinging to each other. At the road, Mark and Charles struggled to get the bodies of Huey and Vince into the bed of the truck. Once loaded, Charles drove the truck up behind the barn while Mark followed in the Lincoln, trying not to look at the body next to him. Once the Lincoln and the bodies were out of sight, Charles took Jodi to the main house and covered her with a blanket on the couch next to the fire. She protested, but he told her she was safe alone for a few minutes while they pulled the Volvo out of the ditch.

Using the tractor, the two men had the Volvo out and hidden behind the barn in minutes. Returning to the main house, Charles saw Jodi standing by the window, watching their every move. She rushed back into his arms the second he stepped onto the porch.

"Everything's going to be okay," he told her again as they held each other on the porch. She jumped slightly when Mark walked around the corner of the house, coming out of the darkness. "It's all right. I want to introduce you to Mark Mulligan. He owns the Big Sky and he's a good friend of mine. He's also one hell of a marksman. Great shot. I owe you big time!"

Jodi didn't respond. "I've heard a lot about you," said Mark in a calming voice. "Will never told me you had the ability to make such a spectacular entrance," he said with a guarded laugh. "Let's get in, out of the cold. I could sure use a drink."

As they walked into the house, Jodi looked at Charles, silently asking herself, "Who's Will?"

He walked her to the couch and wrapped a blanket around her before sitting next to her in front of the fire. Mark delivered three glasses of good whiskey to the coffee table and sat across from them. Charles leaned forward, picking up two, and tried to hand one to Jodi. She shook her head, not saying a word. He had never known her to turn down a drink, but he also recognized that she had just driven twenty-four hundred miles by herself and survived perhaps the most traumatic experience of her life.

"I've got three bodies and two cars I need to make disappear," said Charles before taking a sip of his whiskey. "Any suggestions?"

Mark held his drink with a contemplative look on his face. "I'll have to think about that a bit. I feel kind of bad. We weren't very hospitable after all the miles those guys had come. They'll be fine sleeping outside tonight, and we'll figure out something in the morning. Listen, I want you two to spend the night in the guest room, here in the house, in case any more goombahs come poking around." He took another drink before standing and saying, "I'll put together something for dinner."

While Mark worked in the kitchen, Charles and Jodi sat on the couch near the fire. Jodi was clearly traumatized by the events of the last thirty minutes. She said almost nothing while her husband held her tight. She ate only a few bites of the dinner that Mark had prepared.

Mark volunteered to sleep in the recliner, where he could listen for anybody approaching the ranch. He gave Charles a shotgun and a pistol to set next to their bed, telling him to shoot anybody who came into the house, except himself. "Make damn sure it isn't me, then keep pulling the trigger until they go down."

Charles woke the next morning at dawn to the sound of a tractor outside. He carefully slid out of bed, trying not to wake Jodi. With the pistol in hand, he stepped into the living room. The coffee was on, but Mark wasn't there. He glanced outside and spotted Mark working on the backhoe near the barn in the growing light and falling snow. Charles pulled on his jeans and his boots, then grabbed his hat and his jacket, which were both hung near the door. After stuffing the pistol into his waistband, he picked up the 30-30 before walking down to the barn.

"I'm glad you're here," said Mark as he shut down the backhoe. "I thought we'd bury those three bastards right here, next to the barn." Mark had already dug three shallow graves. "If we get this done right away, the snow will probably keep the fresh dirt covered for months. I need your help moving them, especially that fat kid."

As they went about the gruesome task of moving the three frozen and rigid bodies to the holes, Mark outlined his idea surrounding the disposal of the cars. He knew Reggie, the owner of the wrecking yard near the airport. He'd give him a call and see if they could make the cars disappear for good at the hands of their crusher or their disassemblers. If that didn't work, he'd figure out a way to drop them into the bottom of Flathead Lake. "It's over three hundred feet deep. Nobody's going to be very excited to look for them that far down."

After finishing the task of burying the bodies, they walked back to the main house, where Charles was surprised to find Jodi sitting on the couch, covered in a blanket with a catatonic look on her face. While Mark put breakfast together, Charles held his quiet wife. Just as Mark announced that breakfast was ready, the snow stopped falling and the sun came out, revealing the valley below in all its glory.

Wrapped in her blanket, Charles led Jodi out onto the porch, where they gazed west, across the snow-covered valley. While they stood there, the clouds parted, and the sun shined on the Salish Mountains that guarded the west side of the valley. Jodi stared at the scene before her in silence for several minutes before quietly saying, "Wow."

She ate a few bites of her breakfast without saying much, only responding to questions from the two men with simple yes or no answers. Charles helped clean up after they ate, then Mark grabbed his coat and hat, saying he was going to go check around the property.

"That will give Jodi time to tell you her secret," said Mark.

They both looked at the old rancher with questioning expressions. "What secret?" Charles asked Jodi.

She couldn't believe how perceptive the man had been in such a short time. She looked at Charles, then gently putting her hand on the side of his face, said her first real words since arriving, "I'm pregnant."

EPILOGUE

The DiPiero Family would always wonder what became of Frankie, Vince, and Huey. The communications with the boys ended abruptly a few days after the police raids. The family, left to deal with the mounting legal problems, had always assumed they had escaped to some foreign country. They were no longer welcome in Jersey, and several groups, including some family members, wanted their heads. With the disappearance of the brothers and the seizure of the family assets, the power of the DiPiero family quickly faded, creating a vacuum that was quickly filled by a competing mob family. The remainder of the family, those not subject to prison, lived their lives in relative poverty.

The report that Charles' BMW was possibly in the Chicago area was forever lost in a sea of paperwork at the FBI. Charles Tinsley was assumed dead; his name was included on the memorials of those who died on 9/11. Jodi Tinsley's disappearance was suspected to be an act of revenge by the DiPiero family, however, no evidence was ever discovered to link them to her.

Three months after the SEC froze the assets of Charles Tinsley, $1.8 million dollars was mysteriously transferred from an offshore account to Tinsley's investment account. The funds would eventually be distributed to victims of his Pump and Dump schemes.

In the Flathead Valley, a half million-dollar investment into the Big Sky Ranch helped propel it to become one of the best-known breeders of angus cattle in the United States. Will Roy and his wife, Laura, became well known members of the community as their two daughters grew up. The girls, with tremendous parental support, participated in 4-H, played volleyball and basketball, and lived a life far different from the secret lives their parents had known.

Uncle Mark and his new wife, Aunt Brenda, were with the family each step of the way, attending every choir concert, ball game, and livestock showing as the girls grew up.

Charles and Jodi, or Will and Laura as they were known, lived in a home they built on the Big Sky Ranch, just four hundred yards to the northwest of the main house. They were often seen standing on their porch, holding each other as the sun came up behind them, lighting the peaks of the Rocky Mountains on the far side of the valley.

NEW YORK TO MONTANA

Thom Shepherd & Zach Nytomt

Well, he woke up that morning with a price on his head
Them Lincoln Continental New Jersey boys, they wanted to see him dead
On the Queensboro Bridge, running late for work
Running scared and low on hope
When the second plane hit the building
That's when he became a ghost
And he drove and he drove and he drove

From New York to Montana
Slipping through the cracks
New York to Montana
Running hard and never looking back

Made it to Chicago and he got back on the road first daylight of the twelfth
Crossing Minnesota on into North Dakota till he found his way to Kalispell
She put his picture and a flower on the chain link surrounding
That smoldering holy place in the ground
Way too young to be a widow, aw, but little did she know
That better place he was now
Was flying on wings that he found

From New York to Montana, disappeared without a choice
New York to Montana, dying just to hear her voice

How could he imagine he'd make a hand ranching and be riding the fence line at dawn
In no time that number-crunching, paper-pushing, white collar city boy was all but gone.
He'd had enough of waiting and she fainted when she finally heard his voice on the phone

*If they could make it through the winter, then they'd finally be together
and start a new life all on their own*

*Back in Jersey, somehow, they learned he might not be one of the missing
They started tailing Jodi 'cause they knew if it was true that soon she'd be leaving to be with him
In her rearview mirror, all she could see was that sun-painted shrinking skyline
Westbound hammer down no stopping now, with a feeling in the back of her mind
That they might not be far behind
Still she drove on through the night*

*From New York to Montana
White-knuckled hands on the wheel
New York to Montana, hounds of hell nipping at her heels*

*He couldn't wait to hold her, every minute she was closer
If they didn't catch up with her first
When she spotted that Lincoln, her heart started sinking
Things were about to take a turn for the worse
That winter it was hard, but in the time they spent apart
He'd gotten deadeye good with a gun
And when those goombas caught her at the front gate
He picked 'em off one by one
Three shots rang out and it was done
After all those miles that they'd come*

*From New York to Montana
She ran straight into his loving arms
New York to Montana, and today that's still where they are
With two kids and a cattle farm
And three shallow graves by the barn*

www.zachnytomt.com

www.thomshepherd.com

ABOUT THE AUTHORS

CMA of Texas Songwriter of the Year, Thom Shepherd is an Austin-based touring artist who crosses over many genres from country to tropical music. Thom and his Radio Margaritaville hit, "Always Saturday Night," are featured in "The Parrotheads Documentary" with Jimmy Buffett. Thom is the writer of five #1 singles, including "Redneck Yacht Club" and "Riding with Private Malone." Thom tours constantly with his artist/wife, Coley McCabe. Thom is a two-time cancer survivor and the father of two.

Hailing from the small Northern Texas town of Argyle, Zach Nytomt's unique voice and soulful sound has reached beyond the borders of genre & geography. Moving to Austin, he embarked on a journey that has opened doors that have further propelled his career. Nytomt has been invited to put his talents on display at festivals such as the Steamboat Music Festival, performing at the infamous Gruene Hall, as well as securing residencies at multiple venues around Texas. It's safe to assume that Nytomt has big plans and ambitions, ready to take the country by storm.

Bringing his years of experience to the table, author Dan Sullivan does it again, turning the incredible music of Thom and Zach into a hit novel. The writer of hit books such as "The Greatest Patriot," "Tales from the Land of No Mondays," and "The Tales of Tarpon Jim," Sullivan reaches into his past experiences in finance and growing up around ranching to bring a unique realism to *New York to Montana*. Sullivan lives in Boise, ID with his wife and two children.

BOOKS BY DAN SULLIVAN

(Available on Amazon)

Travels with Amy

The Greatest Patriot

Tales from The Land of No Mondays

The Tales of Tarpon Jim

Made in the USA
Columbia, SC
28 January 2019